The Late Mrs. Fonsell

The Late Mrs. Fonsell

VELDA JOHNSTON

A Novel of Suspense

DODD, MEAD & COMPANY
NEW YORK

Printed in the United States of America

To the memory of Frances Riley Schwarz

The Late Mrs. Fonsell

Chapter 1

FOR MORE THAN half my life, I had lived in my Aunt Elizabeth's tall old house near the foot of Howard Street. And yet as I walked along its second floor hall that night—past the red lacquer chest my grandfather had brought by clipper ship from China, past the oval-framed photograph of my handsome father, at rest these past ten years with other Union dead in Oakland Cemetery—I had a sense of unreality, as if it were only in a bad dream that I moved, skirts whispering over the turkey red carpet, toward my aunt's door.

That, I knew, was because I wanted it to be a dream. I wanted to wake to find myself, weak with relief, in my own bed, rather than approaching my aunt's room to tell her that I, who had no husband, would give birth to a child in about seven months.

I stopped before her door, reached out for its china knob, and then, my courage failing me, turned and walked to the long window at the hall's end.

From there I could look across Sag Harbor cove, its rippled surface reflecting the half-moon, to the point of land known as North Haven. It seemed to me that I could almost make out, rising above the near-leafless trees, the steeply pitched roof and railed widow's walk of the Fonsell house. As always, the sight of that house, or even the thought of it, brought me a sense of faint revulsion.

Nor was it just because its walled rear garden had once been the scene of brutal and inexplicable violence. The house in itself was so ugly. Its three stories were built of brick, not pinkish, time-mellowed brick, but brick that remained a harsh red more than forty years after the house had been built. The stucco-coated pillars that supported its peaked porch roof were disproportionately thick. Curved stucco pediments above its front windows gave the impression of hooded eyes. And on its roof, enclosed by the widow's walk, was a domed skylight of milky green glass. Looking at it, one could almost feel that something noxious in the atmosphere of that house had swelled upward, trying to escape through that monstrous green bubble.

Strange to think that in that ugly, memory-haunted house over there my unborn child's father had grown up, tall and strong and golden. And strange to think that Steven's father —my child's grandfather—probably at this moment was somewhere beneath that roof. Perhaps he was still at dinner with Steven's older sister, Ruth, and his still older half brother, Jason. I could visualize that dining room because I had been in that house, for Ruth's twelfth birthday party. I had never gone there again, because one moonlit night a few weeks later Ruth and Steven's mother had met her violent death in that walled garden. After that, few "nice" children were allowed to enter the Fonsell house.

Did Mrs. Fonsell's portrait still hang above the dining room fireplace? Probably. Ephraim Fonsell was anything but a sensitive man. Of course, hard up as he was these days, he might have sold it. It had been painted, not by one of the itinerant artists who had painted bygone members of my own family, but by a famous and expensive New York artist, John R. Solum. Anyway, I could picture Ephraim Fonsell at the long table of Philippine mahogany, one blunt-fingered hand reaching out for the wine decanter. I could imagine Ruth watching her increasingly drunken father with the odd little smile which her fine-featured face almost always wore, and which, even when we were both children, had held the power to chill me.

Jason would be watching too. Perhaps his eyes showed the sardonic amusement they had held that afternoon last September up at Oakland Cemetery, when he had come upon Steven and me, standing locked in each other's arms inside the inadequate screen of a weeping willow's trailing branches. As we broke apart, Jason had smiled and said, "Sorry to spoil the pretty picture. But you're damn young fools, you know."

From the corner of my eye I had seen that Steven's hands had clenched into fists. "Mind your own business."

Jason's heavy dark brows arched in mock surprise. "But little brother! This is my business. Do you want to get the Fonsells even deeper into the town's black books? That's no wayside bloom you're trying to gather in. If you start fooling around with girls like Irene, every stiff-necked Presbyterian in town will—"

"Shut up!" Steven took a step toward the shorter man. "I know why you followed me."

"I didn't follow you. I was passing along the sidewalk and I looked in here and saw you, the way anyone might have, you young fool."

"I know what's bothering you," Steven went on, as if his brother hadn't spoken. "I've seen you look at Irene."

Jason's dark face flushed. Then he shrugged. "Why not? I like to look at girls. But Irene's in no danger from me. I have another and quite adequate arrangement."

He did, too. The whole town knew about Jason Fonsell's arrangement. Turning, he walked away down the long path that led to the cemetery gates.

Now—and for the first time during these past anxiety-racked weeks—I thought of my unborn child's strangely divided heritage. On my side, ancestors who had settled in Sag Harbor almost a hundred and fifty years before, endured the brutalities of Major Cochrane during the British occupation in 1777, helped repel British gunboats during the War of 1812, and prospered modestly in the years since as

3

professional men, skilled craftsmen, and officers and crewmen of Sag Harbor whalers and merchant ships.

And on Steven's side? Ephraim Fonsell, once one of the richest men on eastern Long Island, but now an aging man sunk deep in drink and debt. Jason Fonsell, illegitimate son of the woman Ephraim had brought back from the California gold fields, a woman he turned out of his house shortly before he married the lovely and tragically fated creature whose portrait might or might not still hang above the dining room fireplace. And Ruth Fonsell, the dead woman's daughter. Strange Ruth, so strange that even though she was twenty-two and beautiful, no man had come courting her.

And the evil rumors that had swirled around that house across the cove after Mrs. Fonsell's death. Whether true or false, they too would be part of my child's heritage.

But thought of the other Fonsells had never shadowed those hours—those pitifully few hours—when Steven and I lay in each other's arms. To me, at least, nothing had mattered but Steven, and the future that had seemed to stretch before us, shimmering with happiness and love.

Over across the cove, lamplight suddenly bloomed in the window of a top floor room under that steep roof. Who was in that room? Some member of the family? No, since it was on the third floor, which once had housed a numerous domestic staff, that room was probably occupied by Annabelle Clyssom, the "arrangement" Jason had mentioned that day up at the cemetery.

I cried silently, "Oh, Steven!" How could it be that he was gone, while those other Fonsells, not one of them worth a hair of his head, still moved about under that steeply pitched roof over there?

But he was gone. And now I had to think of his child, our child, whose coming I must prepare for, somehow.

Turning, I walked to my aunt's door.

Chapter 2

SHE LOOKED UP from her Bible, her thin face between its smooth wings of still-ungrayed hair holding surprise and faint annoyance. All her adult life she had set aside the hour before bedtime for a solitary reading of three chapters from a book of the Old Testament, three from a book of the New Testament, and, finally, her favorite Psalms.

"What is it, Irene?"

Again my courage deserted me. "I have something to talk over, but it can wait."

Her gaze sharpened. Then she said, "Very well. Sit down," and returned her attention to the book, covered in worn calf-skin, which she held on her lap. As I sank onto a straight chair, I noticed with cowardly relief that she was still reading from the Old Testament—from Leviticus, probably, since the page from which she read appeared to be only about a tenth of the way through the heavy volume. Leviticus had many long chapters.

I looked at her, sitting very erect in a mahogany-framed brown velour armchair. It was her fine carriage, as well as her air of quiet dignity, which made people forget that she was really a small woman, only five feet two inches in height. She wore one of the dark bombazine dresses to which she always changed after our midday meal. Tonight it was a bottle-green one, with my Grandmother Haverly's cameo fastened at the high neckline. As she sat there, faith and uprightness seemed to emanate from her, almost as palpably as the scent of patchouli emanated from the Fonsells' boldly handsome housekeeper, Annabelle Clyssom.

I knew that in her undemonstrative way my aunt loved me, just as she had loved her sister-in-law, my mother, a frail woman a generation younger than herself. A true Haverly, she had proved that love with deeds, not words. After the War Department telegram about my father's death had arrived—I was nine then—she had come to our little Rysam Street house and stayed there for a week, supervising the not-very-competent young girl who was the only household help we could afford, seeing to it that I ate properly and said my prayers, and reading the more comforting Psalms to my mother, whose thin face, pink of cheek and brilliant of eye, bore the deceptively healthy-looking marks of lung fever.

When at last my mother was calm enough to listen, Aunt Elizabeth submitted her plan for us. We were three lone females. Of my Grandfather Haverly's five children, only Aunt Elizabeth, the eldest, still lived in Sag Harbor. My father, who had been the youngest, was dead at Chancellorsville, a place I had never heard of until the telegram came. My Aunt Prudence, the next youngest, was down in Savannah, married these past twenty years to a planter who had come to eastern Long Island several years before the Civil War to visit a cotton mill. My two uncles were still out in California where, along with other Long Island gold seekers, they had gone in 1849. Neither of them had found gold, but they had found means of livelihood, and had acquired wives and children. It was not likely, Aunt Elizabeth said, that either of them would return to Long Island. As for my mother's parents, I had never known them. Middle-aged when their only child, my mother, was born, they had died before my own birth.

And so, my aunt said, would it not be best that we three live together? My mother could sell the Rysam Street house.

The proceeds, plus dividends from some railroad shares my father had owned, would bring her enough for clothing and other small necessities. As for food and shelter, she would be glad to have us live in her Howard Street house, that three-story house which Grandfather Haverly, sure by then that she would never marry, had left to Aunt Elizabeth, along with most of the rest of his estate.

We had moved into this house. And here, five months later, my mother had died, with such a peaceful look on her face that I knew, even in my wild young grief, that she had welcomed relief from the burning fever, and from the cough which had racked her for so long.

From that day on, quietly but when need be, sternly, Aunt Elizabeth had seen to it that I ate healthful foods, did my lessons neatly, correctly, and with dispatch, and went with her each Sunday to the tall-spired Presbyterian Church—which people recently had begun to call the Old Whalers' Church—and sat properly gloved and hatted, properly sober of face, beside her in the Haverly pew.

A rustling noise as my aunt turned a page. How handsome, I thought, she once must have been. How handsome she still was, there with the light from the oil lamp shining through its flower-painted globe onto her smooth dark hair and her classic features—the aquiline nose with high-cut nostrils, the firm mouth and chin whose line had softened only a little in the past few years. So many people must wonder why Elizabeth Haverly had never married.

One day shortly after I came to live in this house, I had asked her why she had not. She answered, "Because the only man I ever wanted to marry didn't ask me." Her reply had come promptly, and yet with a firmness that made me realize, young as I was, that the subject was closed.

From then on I wondered about it, though. Which of the men who appeared to me to be about my aunt's age might have married her, if he had wanted to, and had known that

7

he could? Our minister, who had a wife and three grown sons? Our stout and tart-tongued doctor, Doctor Cantrell, whose wife was dead? Or had he been some tragically romantic figure? Perhaps he had been a handsome young whaleship captain back in the eighteen thirties or eighteen forties, who had died and been buried somewhere in the vast reaches of the Pacific.

Well, his identity no longer mattered to me. What mattered was that she was a maiden lady. Except for her father and brothers, it was almost certain that no man had even kissed her cheek. What could she know of the fever in the blood? How could she even understand Steven and me, let alone forgive?

My aunt closed her eyes for perhaps a minute. Even though her lips did not stir, I knew that she was praying. Then, with the thin pages rustling in the stillness, she turned to the New Testament.

Chapter 3

I CANNOT REMEMBER a time when I did not know Steven Fonsell. As young children—he was a year older than I—we both attended the schoolhouse on lower Main Street. But in those days he meant nothing to me. He was just another boy, one of those rough, noisy, untidy creatures whom God had chosen to put upon this earth, although for the life of me I could not think why.

When I was twelve, Aunt Elizabeth enrolled me at a "young ladies' academy" in the nearby village of Bridgehampton, driving me there over the toll road each morning, and fetching me in the afternoon. She could easily have afforded a coachman to drive our surrey, just as she could have afforded a more fashionable vehicle. Under her management, the Haverly money had more than doubled since my grandfather had left it to her. But to Aunt Elizabeth, who handled old Toby's reins skillfully and with enjoyment, keeping a coachman would have seemed a useless and even wicked ostentation.

At the academy the Misses Pride—there were three of them —taught me English composition, American history, advanced arithmetic, and penmanship. I also learned how to paint china, do needlepoint, and properly introduce the President of the United States to the Representative of a Foreign Power, should that task ever fall to me. By my second year there I had developed, along with my classmates, a giggling interest in boys. But my interest centered on no particular boy among those I encountered at Halloween and Christmas parties and Sunday School picnics.

One summer afternoon in my sixteenth year, my aunt and I emerged from the general store onto Main Street's wide sidewalk. Riding up the street on a bay gelding was Steven Fonsell. He reined in. "Good afternoon, Miss Haverly." Then his blue eyes moved to me. "Hello, Irene." I looked at him, at the sun-streaked blond hair, the golden-tan face, the tall figure that sat the restive horse so easily. And I saw that by some mysterious alchemy this boy whom I had known all my life had been transformed into a dazzling stranger. And as we smiled at each other, I saw that his eyes, too, held a look of wondering discovery.

Aunt Elizabeth took my arm. "Come, Irene," she said sharply. "We have more shopping to do."

Feeling as if I moved through a golden haze, I accompanied my aunt while she bought twelve yards of dress material, lightweight gingham of the sort she wore on summer mornings, and placed our packages in the surrey's rear seat. We drove home, past the business buildings of wood or brick, past the beautiful big frame houses on upper Main Street—built by whaleship masters, and therefore known collectively as Captains' Row—and then turned onto Howard Street. When we entered our tall old house she said, "I want to talk to you."

She did, in the small sitting room next to our seldom-used parlor. "Surely I don't have to tell you that you must have nothing to do with the Fonsell family."

That moment on the sidewalk had rendered me rebellious. "Why? Because some people say Mr. Fonsell killed his wife? The coroner didn't say so. He said, 'Person or persons unknown.'" Apparently I had become sanctimonious as well as rebellious, because I added, "I don't think it's very Christian to say such things about him."

My aunt answered composedly, "Perhaps not. But it would be even less Christian to allow you to turn your thoughts in a disastrous direction. Everyone knows that Ephraim Fonsell has become drunken and improvident. Everyone knows that he lived in open concubinage with that poor woman, Jason's mother."

I stood silent, my thoughts diverted momentarily to the woman Ephraim Fonsell turned out of the house before he married his beautiful wife. Jason's mother was still alive, people said, in a tiny village thirty miles to the west.

"And there's Jason himself," my aunt went on. "Could you ever imagine allying yourself with a family that includes a man like him?"

"Why? Because he goes to sea?" For the past two years Jason had been first mate on a brig plying the Australian and Pacific Islands trade. "Men in our family went to sea. What's wrong with that?"

"Nothing. The sea is an honorable calling, for those willing to resist its temptations. Jason isn't one of them. Even when he's at home it's a case of like father, like—"

She broke off. She had not hesitated to mention Ephraim Fonsell's unhallowed alliance, perhaps because of the unfortunate fact that the product of that alliance, Jason, had been a part of Sag Harbor since several years before my own birth. Jason's mode of living, though, was something to be kept from me until I reached a suitable age for such revelations.

But the ears she addressed were less innocent than she supposed. The girls at the academy, in pleasantly shocked whispers, discussed Jason and the woman, five years his senior, who kept house for the Fonsells. If Ruth Fonsell, once an academy student but now graduated, knew that we discussed her illegitimate half brother, her lovely face with its little cat's smile had given no sign. Already tall as an adult, she sat composed and meticulously neat in class, apparently liking no one and liked by no one—not even, I suspect, by the Misses Pride, although they often held up to us as an example Ruth's copperplate penmanship and faultless needle-work.

I cried, "But what's this to do with Steven? Nobody's ever said a word against Steven. You can't blame him for—"

"Irene, by the time you're old enough to marry, you'll realize that you can't marry just a man. You marry his family too. Now the subject is closed. I don't forbid you to greet Steven if you happen to meet him. But after that, walk on. No conversation. And never look at him as you did today, or allow him to look that way at you." Her voice softened. "Will you promise me that?"

Tight-lipped, I looked at her silently for a moment, and then said, "I promise."

For a while I kept my promise, or at least part of it. Whenever Steven and I met—and it seemed to me that we were always meeting, on the street, or in the post office, or some shop—I would answer his greeting and then move on. But in the second or so we were face to face, I could never deny myself the sweet shock of allowing his blue eyes to look directly and deeply into mine. And in church with my aunt on Sundays, aware of Steven sitting alone in the Fonsell pew, I would turn my gaze from the surpliced figure in the pulpit to the stained-glass window in the west wall, so that I could feel Steven's gaze on my profile.

It was three weeks before my graduation from the academy that my aunt told me, as we drove home along the turnpike, that Steven had left Sag Harbor.

I had been thinking about him at that very moment, but that was scarcely a coincidence, since he was often in my thoughts. I was seventeen now, with my education almost completed. A year from now I would be able to consider myself a grown woman. And surely my aunt would acknowledge that a grown woman had the right to follow her inclinations.

My aunt said, "I have something to tell you. Steven Fonsell has gone away."

My heart seemed to stop for a moment, and then begin to thud almost as loudly as the clop of Toby's hoofs.

"He signed on the *Phalarope*." That was the ship upon which his half brother Jason sailed as first mate. "It left at noon today."

Eight months. The voyage to Australia and the Pacific Islands and back always took at least eight months. Anguish seemed to blur my vision, so that the dogwood blossoms on either side of the road looked more than ever like snow flurries, drifting down among the still-curled buds of maples and oaks. Why hadn't he contrived a way of saying goodbye to me? After a moment I realized why. My aunt's opposition to him had been obvious. He had not wanted to risk strengthening that opposition, thus making it even more difficult for us to see each other later on.

"I'm sorry," she said, in a tone that told me she somehow knew about the looks exchanged for several seconds too long, and the proffered profile in church. "But within a few months you will be glad you have had this opportunity to turn your thoughts in some more suitable direction."

My thoughts would not turn. And when the *Phalarope* came back I would see Steven. Alone.

But I did not see him. Typhoid broke out in our village that following winter, and I was one of its victims. For more than two weeks I was aware only of fever, the bitter taste of medicine, and, occasionally, Dr. Cantrell's broad, worried face bending over me. The morning came, though, when I awoke weak but clear-headed. Rose Murphy, my aunt's housekeeper for many years and a valued friend to both of us, spooned broth into my mouth. When she set the bowl aside, I asked her if the *Phalarope* had returned.

"Yes. It's been here, and sailed."

From the sympathy in her round face, I knew that Steven must have sailed with it. Still I asked, "Did Steven Fonsell—"

"Yes, love. He signed on again. His brother didn't."

After a moment I asked dully, "Why didn't he?"

She shrugged. "Who knows about that one? People say he's trying to borrow money for some sort of scheme or another."

So I would have to wait again, until September at the earliest. But perhaps it was just as well he had not seen me. I must look . . . "Rose, could you hand me my mirror?"

She hesitated, then walked to the dressing table and returned with my ivory-backed hand mirror. "Now don't you go fretting. It'll grow back," she said, and left the room.

Appalled, I stared at my thin white face, at my once thick dark hair which had grown sparse, and in spots even vanished. Yes, it was just as well he hadn't seen me.

My hair did grow back, as thick as ever, and more curly. By late winter I felt well enough, and sufficiently presentable, to resume attendance at church and Sunday School and parties. Several young men asked to call. Aunt Elizabeth welcomed each of them, told us that Rose would bring sandwiches and lemonade into the parlor after a while, and then retired to the sitting room, with the door left only a little way open. Her obvious hopes made me feel both sorry for her and guilty, but they did not change my mind and my heart. Each time I went to the post office my pulse raced with the hope that there would be a letter from Steven. There never was.

Nor did the *Phalarope* return in September. Then, one morning in late October, I opened the Sag Harbor *Express* and read: "Word has come that the brig *Phalarope*, out of Sag Harbor, has had bad luck. She ran aground on the Metcalf Reefs, but managed to float free after unloading ballast.

Manning pumps night and day, her crew brought her into Sydney Harbor. The *Phalarope* will be in drydock there for considerable time."

Considerable time. What did that mean? No matter what it meant, even after the *Phalarope* left Sydney it would take her months to cross the vast Pacific, skim through the Straits of Magellan with the Cape Horn gales at her stern, and sail up the coasts of South and North America to anchor beside the Long Wharf of our village. Now I could understand how grimly patient some of the women of my aunt's generation must have felt, waiting two years or more for their menfolk to return from whaling voyages.

Winter came, with northwesterly gales so strong that wind-driven waters of the bay swept up lower Main Street, extinguishing basement furnaces in business establishments, and leaving the occupants to shiver. But gradually the days grew longer and milder, and the trailing branches of willow trees along Main Street's sidewalks sprouted leaves, yellowish at first and then turning the silver-green of full summer.

The day that Steven came back, I was not thinking of him at all. Five miles away from Sag Harbor, I was moving among the dunes that border the beach at Sagaponack, intent upon filling a pail with wild beach plums, so that Aunt Elizabeth and Rose and I could add plum jelly to the rows of preserves we placed on cellar shelves each fall.

As I knelt there in the hollow between two dunes, a cool shadow fell across my body in its white shirtwaist and blue cotton skirt, and across my hands busy among the stiff branches of a plum bush. I turned. There he was atop a dune, standing tall, and broader of shoulder than I remembered, against the blue September sky.

I don't remember getting up. I just found myself standing. "Hello."

"Hello, Irene."

"So you're back."

"Yes. We docked this morning."

"You look older."

"So do you. And prettier. Your hair's different."

"It came out. I had typhoid."

"I know. People told me before I sailed this last time."

Out of conversation, we stood looking at each other. At last he said, "Do you want to sit beside the water for a while?"

I picked up my pail of beach plums. He reached his hand down to help me up the gentle slope. Did he too, as our palms touched, feel a tingling sensation run up his arm?

On the beach we sat, not touching, and watched the rollers topple on a hidden sandbar and rush foaming to shore. I asked, "Will you sign on again?"

"No, at least not for the next trip. Jason thinks I may be able to help him with his plans."

I asked, caring little about the answer, really caring only that Steven would be here for a time, "What plans?"

"Big ones. He wants to buy a ship and start up the sugar trade between Sag Harbor and the West Indies again."

"I see." Vaguely I remembered hearing that Jason Fonsell, of all people, had approached the bank and several of the richer men in town and asked them to set him up in some sort of shipping venture.

"He can't get backing in Sag Harbor. But there's this rich cousin in New York, a cousin of my mother's. He's no relation to Jason, of course, so Jason thinks I might have better luck with him."

Was that Jason's only reason for thinking Steven might have better luck? Or did he realize that Steven had certain qualities—good looks and friendliness and unmistakable candor—which he himself lacked?

We went on talking. About the storms that had battered Sag Harbor the previous winter. About his long voyage. Despite the mishap on the Metcalf Reefs, the voyage had been profitable. Insurance had covered the damage to the ship. Thus the full profit from the cargo delivered at Sydney —Long Island timber, and hides of Long Island cattle—had been split among the ship's owners and its officers and crew. There would be additional money as soon as the return cargo of Australian wool was sold. We talked, too, of young people we had both grown up with. But I felt that beneath the proper conversation we carried on, with a prim two feet of beach sand separating us, we were saying quite different things.

At last he asked, "How old are you now?"

"I was nineteen last May. You're twenty-one, aren't you?"

He nodded. "I turned twenty-one five weeks ago. We were off the Brazilian coast then."

For a while we silently watched a sandpiper who raced after a withdrawing wave to gather tiny crustaceans in its slender beak. Then I said, "You never wrote to me."

"I was afraid of causing trouble between your aunt and you. I was afraid of making it all the harder to see you when I got back." He paused, and then said rapidly, "But I wrote you letters in my head. You'll never know how many. At night, when I was standing lookout. And all during those weeks in Sydney. I thought of you so much that sometimes it seemed to me we weren't separated at all."

So he too had carried on an endless dialogue in his mind. He too had had that sense of closeness which I had felt, lying awake at night and imagining what we would say when we saw each other again.

He asked, "Will it be all right if I call on you?"

I felt the leap of the pulse in the hollow of my throat. Perhaps it was different in big cities. But here on eastern Long Island such a request was tantamount to a declaration of intentions.

"Soon you can. But not right away. My aunt isn't well." Late in July she had suffered a mild stroke. Until Dr. Cantrell pronounced her fit again, I could not ask her to admit Ephraim Fonsell's son, Jason Fonsell's brother, to her house as my suitor.

A dune's shadow touched my shoulder. "I must go home. Aunt Elizabeth will be worried."

In silence we walked over the dunes to where I had left the surrey, on a rutted road leading across level fields to the Bridgehampton–Sag Harbor Turnpike. Near the surrey stood Steven's bay horse, hitched to a split-rail fence.

I asked, as he placed the pail of beach plums on the surrey's floorboard, "Did you know you'd find me here?"

"Yes. I met Rose Murphy on Main Street. She told me you had gone to Sagaponack." I thought of how, for at least a second or so before she told him, poor Rose must have felt torn between her loving respect for Aunt Elizabeth and her romantic sympathy for me.

When I was seated in the surrey with the reins gathered in my hands, he said, still standing in the road, "I think I'll stay here for a while."

With my eyes I thanked him for his understanding. It would not do to have someone tell my ailing aunt that I had been seen on the public road with Steven Fonsell's bay trotting beside the surrey.

We said goodbye, with neither of us, apparently, feeling the need to say we would see each other soon. We knew we would. As the surrey carried me toward the turnpike, my spirits seemed to soar into the golden late afternoon light, like the meadowlarks rising from the roadside stubble on their stumpy, triangular wings.

The next day was the anniversary of my Grandfather Haverly's death. Since Aunt Elizabeth felt too unwell to make her annual pilgrimage to Oakland Cemetery, I went there and placed snapdragons and daisies from our front garden on my grandfather's grave. I knelt long enough to say a prayer, and then wandered along a path between the headstones, reading inscriptions with which I had long been familiar. One marked the grave of a captain whose privateer had harassed British shipping during the Revolution. Another inscription, commemorating the death of two young boys whose sailboat had been swamped, spoke bitterly of those who had watched the drowning but "lifted no hand to save."

I was reading the rhymed epitaph of a Portuguese sailor when I became aware that someone stood at the head of the path. Turning, I saw with a dizzying leap of my heart that it was Steven.

We were alone there among the headstones. The distant sidewalk beyond the iron picket fence was empty of pedestrians. As we looked at each other through the afternoon light, I knew that my face, like his, was saying all that neither of us had said the day before. We moved toward each other. Taking my hand, he led me between the graves to a willow tree. There, in the shelter of its trailing branches, we went into each other's arms. His lips, warm on mine, made me feel more alive than ever in my life before.

He raised his head and laid his cheek against my hair. "Say you'll marry me. You don't have to say when. Just say you will."

"Of course I'll marry you."

We kissed again. And then as we stood there embraced, my head against his shoulder, I became aware of Jason Fonsell, standing just outside the filmy umbrella of the willow. I heard him say, as Steven and I broke apart, "Sorry to spoil the pretty picture. But you're damn young fools, you know."

A few minutes later, after Jason's wide-shouldered figure had disappeared through the cemetery gates, Steven said, "Don't mind my brother."

"I don't." How could I mind anything, now?

"He's not a bad sort. It's just that he's pretty bitter about a lot of things."

19

"I can understand that. I'd better leave now, before someone else sees us."

We kissed again, a briefer kiss, I'm certain, than either of us wanted. Then I left him standing there.

I don't know who told my aunt. I am sure it was not Jason. Some busybody, unnoticed by Steven and me, must also have passed along that sidewalk beyond the picket fence. Anyway, two hours after supper that night, as I stood at my bedroom window, staring dreamily out into the warm dark, my aunt called up the stairwell. I was to come down to the sitting room. At once.

As soon as I walked into the little room, I knew that she knew. Her face was so white, and her usually firm voice so shaken, that I felt more alarm on her behalf than on my own and Steven's. "Irene, I have just heard something incredible. You and Steven Fonsell, up at the cemetery today—"

"Aunt Elizabeth, listen!" Words tumbled out of me. We loved each other. We wanted to marry. Steven was a fine man. What did it matter what the other Fonsells were? And anyway, I was nineteen, old enough to have my choice respected.

At last my aunt said, "Before I called you down here, I thought for a while, and prayed. I have a proposal to make to you. You need to get away to think this over. Will you stay with your Aunt Prudence in Savannah for a month? If at the end of that time you still want to marry Steven— well, we'll talk about it again."

I knew what was in her mind. Her sister Prudence had two pretty daughters, one my age, one a year younger. There would be young men around. Gallant Southern men, like the one who had whisked my Aunt Prudence away from a crowd of Sag Harbor suitors.

It would not work, of course. I wanted Steven, and would still want him any number of months or years from now. But how could I refuse my aunt, who all these years had been both mother and father to me? Besides, during my absence she too would have a chance to think, and perhaps reconcile herself to my becoming Steven's wife.

"I'll go to Savannah."

Her face went slack with relief. "A ship of the Hackley Line is stopping here two days from now." Hackley Line ships carried freight and a few passengers from Boston to Jacksonville, stopping at ports along the way, and then sailed south and east to the Caribbean. "I'm sure you can get passage. And it will be a more pleasant journey by sea than by rail."

She was right about that. The long journey over the Long Island Railroad's newly opened Sag Harbor spur to Bridgehampton, and from there to New York, and then south to Savannah, would entail several changes of line. But I am sure that my aunt was considering also that a sea voyage would keep me away from home longer. Since the ship would stop at various Long Island and Connecticut ports, it would take at least three days just to reach New York. After that there would be the leisurely voyage from one port to another down the Atlantic coast before I could even begin my month's visit in Savannah.

"I'll write to your Aunt Prudence tonight." She paused. "It distresses me to think of you making the trip alone, but I still don't feel at all well. And for a number of reasons"—she smiled faintly—"I am not ready to meet my Maker just yet."

I knew that I was one of her reasons. She wanted to stay alive to protect me, since in spite of her careful upbringing I had turned out—or so it must seem to her—both reckless and headstrong.

"I'll have to say goodbye to Steven."

"No! Don't see him. Promise me you won't. You can send him a note by Rose."

Looking at her tense white face, at the shaking hand she raised to her lips, I knew she feared that if I saw Steven, he would persuade me to run away and marry him. Until that moment I had not realized her full horror of the thought that I might ally myself with the family in that North Haven house—a house where, some people persisted in saying, Ephraim Fonsell had battered his beautiful wife to death.

I felt chilled, as if a shadowy something had come to stand between me and the warm lamplight. Then I dispelled it. I would never live in that ugly house with Ephraim Fonsell and his surly elder son and his pale, strange daughter. Never! Steven would not expect or want us to live there. We would live on this side of the cove, perhaps in one of the new little houses that had been built in recent years on Division Street.

My aunt still looked at me, with naked pleading in the eyes that were usually so calm. I said, "All right. I'll send him a note."

I did, the next morning. It said, "My aunt knows about us. She wants me to spend a month with my aunt in Savannah to think things over. I must do it. She isn't well. But I won't change."

Within half an hour, Rose came back with his reply: "I understand. I won't change either. I love you."

Around ten o'clock the next night, a night so foggy that the wooden planks of Long Wharf were pooled with moisture, I boarded the *Amelia Boyce,* a two-hundred-foot sailing vessel with auxiliary steam power, and passenger accommodations for fifteen.

On the opposite side of the room, thin pages rustled as my aunt turned back to the Old Testament. My stomach tightened until I felt almost nauseous. Only the Psalms were left now. Soon I would have to tell her.

Chapter 4

ON THE AFTERNOON of the day the *Amelia Boyce* docked in
New York, I rode up Fifth Avenue in a hired carriage. Beside me sat a fellow passenger, a young matron named Mrs.
Ames, bound for the island of Jamaica, where her brother
and his family lived. An ex-New Yorker married to a Boston
man, Mrs. Ames had taken me under her fashionable and
somewhat giddy wing the day after the ship left Sag Harbor.
Now she excitedly pointed out the dwellings of the fabulously
rich. Not liking what I saw, I stared at the thick traffic of
hackney cabs and private landaus and broughams, at the
top-hatted men and modishly bustled women moving past
the great marble and brownstone houses whose steps rose
directly from the sidewalk. How terrible! How very, very sad
not to have a front lawn.

Vaguely I realized that I should be enjoying this, my second glimpse of New York. My dimly remembered first visit
here had been with my father and mother, when I was five.
But I was too homesick to enjoy myself, and too anxious
about Steven. What if some circumstance impelled him to
go to sea again during my absence? Now that he had held
me in his arms, now that we were pledged to marry, I felt
that I could not endure another long separation.

I was glad when the carriage returned us through the fading light to the ship. And an hour later, as I lay on the bunk
in my small cabin, I was glad to feel the vibration of the
auxiliary steam engine and then the slow movement of the
ship from its berth.

Someone knocked. Rising from the bunk, I lit the lantern which hung in its gimbals on the wall, and opened the door.

Steven stood there in the dimly lighted passage.

I went into his arms. In that first moment, I did not even wonder how he happened to be there. He said, lips close to my ear, "Let's go up on deck."

When we emerged from the steep companionway onto the deck, I saw that the ship, still under steam power, was moving through the Narrows. But as we stood at the rail I was only vaguely aware of Staten Island on our starboard side, its scattered lights blooming through the dusk, and of the few passengers who strolled the deck behind us.

The night after I sailed, Steven told me, he and Jason had agreed that there was no sense in delaying an approach to Steven's rich New York cousin. "I also told him that I might as well go down to the West Indies and talk to some of the sugar planters we'll buy from, if Jason ever gets that shipping line started." This morning he had taken the train to New York, talked to his cousin, whose response was cautiously favorable, and boarded the *Amelia Boyce* a few minutes before it sailed.

"Did Jason know you were going to sail on the same ship as—"

"Maybe he suspected. If so, I don't imagine he liked it. But the only thing that really matters to him is his shipping line. And he needs my help with that. He needs it too much to risk riling me again, the way he did at the cemetery the other afternoon."

His hand tightened over mine as it lay on the rail. "Marry me! The captain can marry us right away, tonight."

I looked up at him, not moving, but with my whole heart and body yearning toward him.

"Your aunt won't have to know, not until you come back from Savannah. And she should be feeling stronger by then.

Please, Irene, please marry me. I've got this awful feeling that if we don't marry now, we never will."

So he had felt it too, that fear of a long or perhaps permanent separation that had weighed upon me as I rode up Fifth Avenue.

I said, "Yes. Yes, darling. Go talk to the captain."

Around nine o'clock that night in the captain's cabin, with an uncomfortably shy third mate and a fluttering Mrs. Ames as witnesses, Steven and I were married. If the captain had been older or more dour, he might have urged us to wait, or even have refused to perform the ceremony. But he was an amiable man of not much more than thirty. Besides, he had no real reason to refuse. Obviously Steven and I were of a legal age to marry.

After the ceremony, I gave the captain back the heavy signet ring which he had stripped from his little finger, so that Steven could place it on my left hand. A few minutes later the captain smilingly handed me the written certification of our marriage, and handed to Steven the key of the double cabin to which the purser had transferred our luggage.

For a moment after Steven had twisted the key in the lock, and turned to face me there in our cabin, I felt a shyness I had never known in all the years I had loved him. Then, as we moved toward each other, every bit of shyness dropped away.

During the next five days while the ship moved slowly south, halting at ports along the way, Steven and I talked very little with other passengers, except at mealtimes. Then we shared a table with Mrs. Ames and the shy third mate, in the dining salon that served both the ship's officers and the passengers. There were fewer passengers now—only eleven —than when the *Amelia Boyce* sailed from Sag Harbor. Six passengers had left the ship in New York, and only two had come aboard there—Steven, and a deaf, tremulous old man who was going to Jacksonville to live with his son. Nor did we pick up additional passengers as the ship discharged and loaded cargo at Baltimore and Norfolk.

Steven and I were glad that there were no new passengers with whom we would have had to chat politely. And we were pleased and grateful that the shipmates we did have left us alone. Perhaps it was not just out of consideration for our newly wedded state that they did so. Except for the old man and me, they were all bound for the West Indies, some on business, some to visit relatives, some just for a leisurely cruise of the islands. Their common destination seemed to focus their interest upon each other, so that they were almost like members of a private yachting party.

Whatever the reason, Steven and I were left alone to stroll the deck, to stand at the after rail watching the ship's glassy, foam-flecked green wake, and, when the fancy took us, to retire to our cabin in broad daylight. Not all of our hours there were spent in lovemaking. Often we lay quietly talking of our future, of the small Sag Harbor house we would rent, or perhaps even buy, and of the proposed Fonsell Shipping Line and its chances of success.

During one such interlude I learned that Jason's ambitions were even larger than I had realized. "He wants to start his own sugar refinery, too. He has the site picked out, on Bay Street."

I wondered why he hungered so after success. Was he just greedy for what riches could buy? Or did he relish the thought that one day, made powerful by success, he would be able to refuse or grant favors to the men who had denied him financial backing?

When the ship reached Savannah, Aunt Prue met me in her coachman-driven carriage. Even though Steven and I had said our long and impassioned goodbyes the night before, I could not resist turning, as the carriage drove away from the dock, to wave to the tall young figure beside the ship's rail.

26

Aunt Prue asked, twirling the handle of the parasol that shielded her dark ringlets, "Who was that you waved to, sugar?"

Although plumper, Aunt Prudence was almost as handsome as I remembered her from her last visit to Sag Harbor, when I was a small child. But in the intervening years her Yankee accent had taken on an added Southern softness, just as her complexion had acquired an added Southern creaminess—which, Aunt Elizabeth had once remarked, probably came more from eating all that gravy and hot bread than from staying out of the sun.

"He was just a passenger," I said. Aunt Prudence must not know, lest she feel it her duty to write to Sag Harbor.

Lonely as I was for Steven, I liked Savannah. I liked its warm, flower-scented nights and its sultry days, when my aunt and her two daughters, wearing light wrappers over their petticoats and camisoles, moved languidly about the spacious house in the dim, subaqueous light that filtered through the green jalousies. I liked Aunt Prue's husband. Even though he spent most of his evenings in the bar of Savannah's best hotel, whenever he was at home he treated his wife with a flattering courtliness that would have moved any long-married Yankee husband to ribald mirth.

I also liked the deep, pillared porch of my aunt and uncle's house. Each night on that porch my pretty cousins, their daytime languor transformed to liveliness by the cooler air and the presence of several young gentlemen callers, laughed, flirted, and sang duets to the accompaniment of my elder cousin's mandolin. The young men were as gallant to me as they were to Jocelyn and Dorothea. Aware as I was almost every waking moment of Steven, I at first had a sense of receiving their attentions under false pretenses. But soon I realized that when a Southerner intimates that with the slightest encouragement he will throw himself at your feet, you are in little danger of looking down to find him there. He's just being polite.

One morning during my third week in Savannah, I awoke to find wind and rain assaulting the house with almost tropical fury. I also awoke to the faint anxiety, not untinged with delight, which had weighed upon me for several days now. But probably, I told myself, as I looked at the writhing limbs of a pepper tree beyond the streaming windowpane, I had no cause for either anxiety or delight. Probably it was just the stress and excitement of these past weeks.

Six mornings later I left my room to go down to breakfast. Today I would not dawdle over the hot biscuits, the grits, and shirred eggs. The *Sea Sprite,* the ship upon which I had reserved passage home, was due in Savannah the next day, and I wanted to do some last-minute shopping before I sailed.

I had descended only a few steps of the stairs when the front door opened and Dorothea, my younger cousin, came in. She held the morning newspaper in one hand. "Oh, Irene! Were you ever lucky!" Her upturned face held mingled dismay and excitement. "Not to have stayed on that ship, I mean."

I stopped short, clutching the banister rail. I said, in a voice I would not have recognized, "What—"

"You know that bad storm we had last week? It was the edge of a Caribbean hurricane. The *Amelia Boyce* went down in it."

After a moment I managed to say, "The passengers?"

"Everyone aboard was lost. The ship sent up rockets, and another ship got close enough to see the *Amelia* going down, and people struggling in the water, but the storm was so bad they couldn't launch life— Irene! What is it?"

I had turned. A gray mist was closing in. I struggled through it to my room and fell face down across the bed.

Dorothea was standing beside me now. "Oh, Irene! If I'd—"

"Please." I reached out a groping hand. "The paper."

When she gave it to me, I ignored the black headline, and tried to focus my suddenly blurred vision on the passenger list, halfway down a column of newsprint. Perhaps he had left the ship before it foundered. But no. His name was there.

I didn't sail the next day. Instead I lay dazed and silent in bed. "Such a shock," Aunt Prue kept saying, as she fussed with window shades, and proffered food I could not eat. "People you knew going down like that." If she remembered that I had turned to wave at one particular passenger, she refrained from mentioning it.

On the following Monday the *Lucy Greene,* a northbound sister ship of the *Amelia,* stopped at Savannah. I sailed on it.

Shortly after dawn eight days later, the ship tied up alongside Sag Harbor's Long Wharf. I was glad that we had arrived early, while the warehouses built out along the wharf were still closed, and Main Street's sidewalks still empty. At this hour there was no one to watch me descend the gangplank except Aunt Elizabeth, in the rear seat of the surrey, and our part-time handyman, Pete, in the driver's seat.

Pete hurried forward to take my luggage from the crewman who carried it. In my absorbing grief I did not recognize the significance of the fact that my aunt, who had always handled the reins with so much pride and pleasure, had needed someone to drive her the short distance from our house to the wharf.

As I approached the surrey, I saw shock in her face. I did not wonder at it. I knew I looked awful. During the northbound voyage I had eaten little and slept even less.

Aunt Elizabeth did not kiss me. She wasn't the kissing type. But as we drove along Main Street she said with a tremor in her voice, "I'm so terribly sorry. I mean, I can see you know about Steven."

"Yes."

"When your Aunt Prudence wired that you were taking a later ship, I guessed that you had read about it in the papers."

"Yes."

She didn't speak again until the surrey was approaching our corner. Then she said, "I must ask you this. Before you left home, did you and Steven arrange that he was to board your ship in New York?"

"No." It was such an effort to speak. "The idea didn't come to him until after I had left here."

"I see. Forgive me for thinking that you might have deliberately deceived me, but I had to make sure." We turned onto Howard Street. "The whole town is sorry about Steven. Everyone liked him." Her voice shook. "It was my fault. If I hadn't persuaded you to go away, he wouldn't have followed you."

I aroused myself sufficiently to say, "You couldn't have known what would happen. It was no one's fault."

I could not summon up the energy to tell her the whole truth. Nor had I told her during these past ten days—days in which, unwilling to face the townspeople, I had kept close to the house, and retreated to my room with the plea of "feeling tired" whenever I glimpsed a visitor coming up the walk. It was true that everyone had liked Steven, but that would not have prevented people from gossiping. Word must have spread that Steven and I had been up at Oakland Cemetery. Everyone must know that I had sailed on the *Amelia Boyce*. And from newspaper accounts of the sinking, everyone also knew that Steven had been listed as a passenger who had boarded the ship in New York.

But all day today I had realized that I must tell my aunt —and *soon*—that although I could think of no quick and easy way to prove that Steven Fonsell had been my husband, I carried his child.

Waiting, I watched my aunt over there across the room, her worn face filled momentarily with the peace that reading the Psalms always brought to it.

Chapter 5

CLOSING THE BIBLE, Aunt Elizabeth placed it on the lamp table. She took off her glasses, restored them to their needle-point case, and laid the case beside the calf-bound volume. "Well, Irene?"

I found I could not speak.

Anxiety sharpened her gaze. "Irene! What is it?"

"I—Steven and I—" My throat closed up.

After about four seconds, I knew she had understood. I knew it by the terror that leaped into her eyes. "Dear God," she said. "Oh, my poor, foolish—" She broke off, and then asked, "When?"

"June, I think." The pressure in my throat eased a little. "It wasn't like that, Aunt Elizabeth. Steven and I were married. The ship's captain married us."

As I went on talking, a little color came back into her face. She said, "You should have told me you were married. You should have told me long before this, by telegram or letter, so that I could tell everyone about it. Now people will think it strange—"

"I wanted to tell you myself," I said dully. "I thought you'd be—much stronger by the time I got back."

But obviously she was not stronger. The news that Steven had been aboard the *Amelia Boyce,* and the consequent gossip, must have taken its toll of her strength. And the sight of me, coming thin and dull-eyed down the gangplank, could not have helped. What was more, during these last ten days, as I had moved listlessly about the house, I had sometimes been aware of increasing worry in her eyes.

Her voice softened. "Yes, I can see why you didn't write to me about your marriage. Now, though, we must tell everyone, right away."

Again I had to force the words out. "But I can't prove it."

She looked incredulous. "Can't prove what? That you and Steven were married? Of course you can. The captain must have given you some sort of certification."

"Steven kept it. I was afraid that if I did Aunt Prue or one of the girls would see it, and then you might hear—"

The fear was coming back into her face. "But there must have been passengers who will remember your marriage, people besides you who left the ship before it went down."

"Six people left it in New York. But that was before Steven even came aboard. And there was an old man who was to leave the ship in Jacksonville. His name was Carter, or Carson, or something like that. We—I didn't pay much attention to the other passengers. He might remember, if we could find him. But I doubt that anyone even told him about Steven and me. He was so very old, and so deaf. The dining room waiters had to lean down and shout in his ear, and other people didn't even try to talk to him."

My aunt's face was deathly white. "But perhaps Steven told people when he went ashore in the islands. He was going to talk to sugar planters, wasn't he? That's what Jason told people."

I too had thought of that. After a search that might prove long and expensive, perhaps we would find someone who could testify to the fact of my marriage—some islander Steven had told about it during a trip ashore, or one of our former shipmates who had disembarked at some Caribbean port before the hurricane struck. I had looked over that list of lost passengers, clipped from the Savannah newspaper, many times, hoping to recall the name of some passenger who was not on the list. But I remembered few names besides that of Mrs. Ames, and all those I did recall, including hers, were on the list of those drowned.

What was more, I would not even know where in the islands to start our search. The *Amelia* had been scheduled to call at more than a half dozen Caribbean ports. I said, with an effort, "I've thought of one thing. We could write to the Hackley Line, and ask them for the names of any passengers who might have left the ship before it went down, and where they left it. Then we could try to get in touch with them—"

But even if the Hackley Line could supply the names of such a passenger or passengers, they might no longer be on the island where they had disembarked. And while we carried on our perhaps vain search, each passing week would make my condition more obvious.

Aunt Elizabeth's thoughts must have followed my own, because she said, in a flat voice, "It's too big a risk. We might spend months, and still not find anyone. We must make some other sort of plan."

Some sort of plan. The one plan I could not make was to stay here. No matter what I told the townspeople, even those most well disposed to me would have their lingering doubts, and others would be sure that my child was illegitimate. For my own part, perhaps I could face them down. But I could not subject my child to the pitying looks of adults, and, later on, the taunts of other children.

I had a sudden memory of how a classmate at the academy had somehow got hold of a copy of *Woodhull and Claflin's Weekly,* the notorious Claflin sisters' newspaper, and brought it to school. Shocked and titillated, we girls read articles which not only advocated votes for women, but prophesied that someday a woman who, either through misfortune or by choice, bore a child out of wedlock would not be looked upon as a criminal outcast. Nor would people think of her child as branded with her shame. Well, perhaps—in a hundred years, say. But this was the fall of 1873. The life of my child, especially if she were a girl, would be shadowed from her first day onward, unless I made sure that she began her life among strangers.

I said, "You could tell people I was going back to Savannah. Then I would go to Chicago or Philadelphia, or some other place where I would be just a young widow—"

"Go away all by yourself, at nineteen? Have your child with no one near you who— No, it's quite impossible." She drew a deep breath. "I see what must be done. I'll empower Mr. Yuill to sell this house and my other property here." Mr. Yuill was her lawyer. "Then we'll go to California—I can say it's for my health—and stay there."

Grateful but appalled, I looked at her white face, at her thin hands which trembled, even though she had clasped them in her lap. Aunt Elizabeth's roots went deep. Her own father had built this house, and she had lived in it all her life. To expect her to live for long in some other place would be like expecting a sick and aging tree to survive transplantation to alien soil.

I said, "I can't ask that of you."

She stretched her lips into a smile. "Why, you know I've always wanted to see California. And your uncles are out there—"

She broke off. I knew that she had remembered that both my uncles had young daughters. My uncles' wives would not welcome the presence of an expectant young relative who had nothing to support her claim of widowhood.

I said, "Let's don't decide tonight."

She nodded. "Better to sleep on it."

Abruptly I got to my feet. "I think I'll take a walk."

Again she nodded. "It would be good for you. You've been indoors too much since you came home."

Wearing a cashmere shawl against the early November

35

chill, I moved up the gentle slope of Howard Street and then turned left onto Captains' Row. How I loved these dignified frame houses, built in the prosperous whaling days before I was born. I loved their columned porches, and their shutters, and their fanlighted doors. Sag Harbor craftsmen had taken pride in making each door, each fanlight, of a different design than any other in town.

How much I loved my whole village, even though its great days seemed gone forever. Aunt Elizabeth was not the only one for whom uprooting would be painful. But I was young, and would survive self-banishment from my birthplace, whereas she . . .

Halfway down the slope that led to lower Main Street, I crossed to the opposite sidewalk and then halted, looking down at the business district. The gas street lamps still burned there, throwing a bluish radiance over the rows of darkened shops, and Nassau House, and the imposing façade of the three-story Huntting Building at the foot of Long Wharf.

Memory stirred in me. The previous February, while I was still waiting for Steven's damaged ship to return from Australia, the new Music Hall in the Huntting Building had been opened with a Grand Ball. Pabst's famous orchestra had been brought all the way from New York. The food, too, had been supplied by a New York caterer.

My hair had grown out sufficiently by then for me to attend, wearing a new dress of pale yellow taffeta. Aunt Elizabeth was there too, of course, in her ten-year-old brown velvet. Our escort, the son of an East Hampton doctor, had been among those who had called upon me that winter.

Late in the evening, as I stood between dances with a group of young people under the brilliant, gas-globed chandelier, I saw Jason Fonsell moving toward us. Even though old Ephraim Fonsell had once been a rich and powerful man in this town, my first thought was surprise that his illegitimate elder son had been invited—or, if invited, had cared to attend. My second thought was, as I saw that his gaze was fixed upon me, "He has a message from Steven!"

He stopped before me, bowed, and said through the opening strains of *Artist's Life*, "May I have this waltz?"

Aunt Elizabeth would not like it. Perhaps she was watching me right now, from across the room where the older women sat. But he must have at least some word of Steven. I uttered the customary formula. "With pleasure."

As he whirled me over the polished floor among the other couples, I asked, "Have you heard from your brother recently?"

For a moment the gray eyes under the heavy brows held no expression. Then he smiled and said, "I thought that was why you were willing to dance with me."

I persisted, "Have you heard from him?"

"A letter came last week. He's still in Sydney."

We did not speak again. In the lengthening silence I became uncomfortably aware of his broad left hand clasping my right one, and of his other hand placed on my back. Even though it rested lightly, it seemed to me that I could feel its warmth through my dress and my camisole and my stays. The sensation was a little frightening. I was glad when the music stopped. He bowed, an ironic little smile curving his mouth with its full lower lip, and walked away.

Now, almost as if the memory had conjured him up, I saw Jason's wide-shouldered figure emerge from a tavern about fifty yards away. Bathed in the glow of a street lamp, he untied a bay horse from a hitching post, mounted, and rode at a brisk trot toward the foot of Main Street. It was Steven's horse. I was sure of it. But then, it must be Jason's horse now. Perhaps everything of Steven's belonged to Jason, as well as most of what Steven, as the younger but legitimate son, would have inherited later on.

Everything that would have been Steven's.

I stood motionless, turning over and over in my mind the idea that had come to me.

More than once these past anxious days I had allowed myself the fantasy that one of the young men who had courted me the previous winter might offer a solution in the form of immediate marriage. But I knew that such thoughts were a waste of time. None of those young men would want to marry me if I told them of my situation. And even if deception were possible, I would not be able to carry it through.

But with a man like Jason, deception would not even be necessary.

It was unthinkable that I, who had lain in Steven's arms, would ever lie in Jason's. It was almost equally unthinkable that I would ever live in that ugly house across the cove with its blood-stained memories. Those would be my first two stipulations.

Even so, I felt reasonably sure that Jason, being Jason, would snap up the bargain that my aunt and I could offer him. Turning, I hurriedly retraced my steps.

I was not surprised to see a ribbon of lamplight under my aunt's door. I had been sure that she would not even try to sleep for many hours. I knocked, and she told me to come in.

For a while as I talked, her face held only horrified opposition. But gradually a considering look came into her eyes.

"Don't you see?" I said. "Fonsell is my child's rightful name. He can be baptized as a Fonsell, with no one daring to raise questions, at least not openly. And right here in Sag Harbor, not three thousand miles away."

"Many people will still think the child is not Jason's."

"Let them. Who can prove it? Legally he will be Jason Fonsell's child, his premature child, and after a few years most people will have forgotten there was ever any doubt about it. It's not a solution I want, God knows. But at least it's better." Better, I meant, than condemning her to loneliness and an unnecessarily early death. Better than finding myself in a strange place, all alone and with a child to raise.

"All right." Her face went slack in capitulation. "I'll go over there and talk to him tomorrow morning."

Chapter 6

DAWN LIGHT HAD begun to fill my room before I fell asleep. Thus I did not hear the surrey move from the carriage house and pass beneath my window. The sound of its return awoke me, though. I rose, and hastily poured water from the china pitcher into the washbasin. I was dressing when my aunt knocked.

"He agreed," she told me, when I had opened the door. In the sunlight streaming through the window behind me, her tired and still anxious face showed at least a little satisfaction in the completion of a painful task. "He'll be here in about an hour."

Forty minutes later, as I sat stiffly on a small red plush chair in the parlor, I heard my aunt admit him to the house. He halted just inside the parlor doorway. Evidently he had ridden the bay mare across the bridge because, in addition to a dark frock coat and trousers and a fawn-colored waistcoat, he wore black riding boots. He said, with a slight bow, "Good morning."

"Good morning." I waved my hand toward a carved mahogany armchair. "Please sit down."

When he was seated he said, "I hope this will not come as a great shock to you, but I am here to ask you to be my wife."

Let him be as sardonic as he pleased. It was preferable to any kind of pretense. I inclined my head. "I will marry you."

"When?"

"As soon as possible. In ten days, say."

"Fine. Under the circumstances, it's good to know that you don't believe in long engagements."

That did sting. Feeling color in my cheeks, I said, "One thing before we go any farther. Do you believe I was married to Steven?"

He said promptly, "I do. But it would make no difference if I didn't. I'd marry Jezebel herself to get my hands on that money."

My aunt's money. The money he would use to buy a ship, and to build his sugar refinery.

I spoke the little speech I had rehearsed. "I hope my aunt made it clear that this will be strictly a marriage of convenience—your convenience and my convenience. I hope she also made it clear that if and when I decide upon divorce, you will make no difficulties." I was sure he would have provided me by then with ample grounds.

"She made it clear, and I agreed. If you find our arrangement intolerable, or if another plumed knight rides into your life, I shan't stand in your way. The contract to be drawn up between your aunt and myself will remain binding. That is, the firm of Fonsell and Haverly will not be dissolved, even if the marriage is."

A plumed knight. I pondered the sardonic phrase. Even now that Steven was dead, did Jason feel any affection for his memory? Or did he feel only envious resentment of the younger, legitimate son whose mother had ousted his own mother from the Fonsell house?

"Then there's only one matter left to discuss," I said. "Where will we live? The old Fotheringay house on Madison Avenue is still for sale. It's quite large." With a stab of pain, I remembered how Steven and I had planned to start our lives together in some small, snug house. "Large enough that we could keep out of each other's way."

"No."

I said, puzzled, "You mean you have some other house in mind?"

"Of course. My house, mine and my father's."

I said, after a speechless moment, "But I can't, I won't!"

He appeared unruffled. "Why not?"

"You cannot expect me to live in the same house with your mistress! What would people say?"

"They won't say anything. By the time you and I are married, Annabelle will have other accommodations."

Nearby accommodations, I was sure. No exile to a remote hamlet for Annabelle, as there had been for Jason's mother. I said flatly, "Even so, I won't live there."

For the first time, he showed a spark of anger. "Why? Because of what happened to my father's wife? You think he may have killed her. Is that it?"

Unable to think of a reply, I remained silent.

"She was killed by an escaped lunatic! The only reason he wasn't indicted is that you can't indict an insane person."

Such a man had figured in the case. Escaping from an asylum in Connecticut, he apparently had stolen a rowboat and crossed the sound to Long Island. Two days after the murder, he was found cowering in a brushy hollow in the Shinnecock Hills. There was blood on his gray asylum uniform, but whether it came from a partially healed cut on his hand, or from the murdered woman, there was no way of telling. The police questioned him about the crime, and showed him the blood-stained pine branch which they had found in the woods near the Fonsell house and which, they were sure, had been used to batter the woman to death. His answers were either confused denials, or a look of complete incomprehension.

"You're not afraid of ghosts, are you?" Jason asked. "Let me assure you, my stepmother doesn't haunt the place."

But the lunatic who might have been her murderer had haunted my childhood dreams. In nightmares he had crouched on a branch overhanging a brick garden wall. Moonlight—the evil moonlight that sometimes illuminates bad dreams—had struck through the leaves to shine on his eyes. Then, panther-like, he had dropped to the ground and raced, with the club in both upraised hands, toward a terror-frozen figure that was not Mrs. Fonsell, but my ten-year-old self.

Jason went on, "Even if my father did it—and he didn't—he won't kill *you*. He's an old man now." As I remained silent, he resumed, "Besides, your aunt can live there with you. You'll be needing her, later on."

I said, "I won't do it. I won't live in that house. I don't see why you insist that I do."

His face flushed. "Then I'll tell you why." He leaned forward in his chair. "I know what people in this town say about my father. I know why neither you nor any of the others at Ruth's birthday party were ever allowed to come to our house again."

So he remembered that birthday party, given a few weeks before Mrs. Fonsell's violent death. I recalled now that I had caught a glimpse of him as he moved along the hall past the dining room where we children ate ice cream and pink birthday cake. But he must have been around eighteen then, an adult to my ten-year-old eyes, and therefore of no interest.

I could not resist saying, "There might have been other reasons why we children weren't allowed in that house."

"No, there weren't, not for another two years, if you're talking about Annabelle and me. She was there then, but as far as I was concerned, she was still only the housekeeper.

"Anyway," he went on, "if I marry, and my wife refuses to live in the Fonsell house, some damn fools will be even more sure that my father is a murderer. They'll think that I have admitted to you that he is. And I just won't have that."

"I don't think people would necessarily conclude that."

"Perhaps not. But if you are willing to live in that house, with my father still there, it will go a long way toward dispelling those old stories. And that's what I want. That's what I expect to get out of this bargain, as well as the money."

"I'm sorry." I really was, in a way. It had never occurred to me that Jason cared what people said of his father. "But I will never live in that house."

He looked at me for a long moment. Then, sighing, he got to his feet. "I'm sorry too. I'll just have to raise the money somewhere else."

I looked at him incredulously. "Where will you raise it? Everyone knows you haven't been able to in Sag Harbor."

"There's still that cousin in New York."

"Steven's cousin! Why should he loan you money?"

"I think he may. According to the letter Steven sent me from New York, his cousin was inclined to regard it as a sound business proposition."

Steven had told me much the same thing. With a little drum of alarm starting up inside me, I wondered if Jason was bluffing. Would he, just because I refused to live in that house, turn down my aunt's offer? After all, he could not be sure that Steven's cousin would back him, not at all sure.

But if he wasn't bluffing, my future and my aunt's and my child's would be as lonely and uncertain as it had seemed the night before. No, worse. If Jason talked, everyone would know that it was not because of my aunt's poor health that we had gone to California. Everyone would know that she had tried to buy me a husband. And even though she would not be here, and even though she would never mention it to me, she would suffer terribly at the thought of what lifelong friends and neighbors were saying. Surely, after all her years of piety, charitableness, and deep if undemonstrative affection for family and friends, she deserved better than that.

He said, drawing a watch from his waistcoat pocket, "Well, there's no point in wasting more of each other's time. And I must get ready for the trip."

The trip to New York.

Steven's cousin probably would refuse to back him.

But he might not.

I could not take the chance. I said, feeling a flash of pure hatred, "Very well. I'll live in that house."

Chapter 7

THE HACKNEY WE had hired after alighting at Sag Harbor depot rattled across the North Haven bridge and then moved briskly along the tree-walled dirt road. Jason and I rode silently side by side, clad in the traveling clothes in which we had left Sag Harbor ten days before, immediately after our marriage.

Held in the parsonage rather than the church, it had been the simplest of ceremonies. The short announcement my aunt had placed in the *Express* gave her ill health as the reason that the marriage would be "strictly private." We had attendants, though. Jason's father, flushed of face but completely sober for the occasion, was best man. My attendant was Ruth Fonsell. Slender and tall—tall as the bridegroom —she had looked eerily beautiful in ice blue taffeta. I was given in marriage by Aunt Elizabeth's physician and lifelong friend, Dr. Cantrell, the only person besides Jason's family and Rose Murphy to whom my aunt had confided the circumstances behind this hasty marriage.

After the ceremony, Aunt Elizabeth and I had returned alone to the Howard Street house. There I had changed from my wedding dress to a brown merino skirt and jacket. I was glad to get out of that dress. Aunt Elizabeth and I had made it, working swiftly and for the most part silently. Looking at her dark head bent above her skillfully plied needle, I had thought often of how distressed she must be by the implicit lie that dress expressed. But for me to have worn anything but bridal white would have lent added weight to the stories we knew must be circulating through town. Thanks to me, I reflected sorrowfully, my aunt's path was no longer determined by a simple choice between right and wrong. Of late she'd had to decide which course represented the lesser evil.

Soon after I had changed to traveling costume, I heard the sound of wheels outside. Looking through the front window, I saw the hired carriage from the depot. I gathered my aunt's thin body in a brief embrace, and then went downstairs to join Jason for our trip to New York.

Few honeymoons, I imagine, have been stranger than Jason's and mine. At our hotel in the Murray Hill district, Jason told the reception clerk that since "Mrs. Fonsell hadn't been sleeping well," we would require separate rooms. During the daylight hours, too, we went our separate ways. I window-shopped in Herald Square, and went to matinee performances of a musical review and of *Camille*. And I spent long hours in my room, reading paperbound copies of Jane Austen's *Persuasion* and Trollope's *Barchester Towers*. As for Jason, I gathered that he passed his days in the financial district, in ship chandler shops along the waterfront, and at a sugar refinery on the New Jersey side of the Hudson.

We had dinner together each night, in the hotel's quietly elegant dining room. There we exchanged brief accounts of our day's activities, and then lapsed into silence. I'm sure that anyone observing us concluded that, despite our youthful appearance, we had been married long enough for acute boredom to set in.

But now that ten-day respite was over. Now, I thought, as the carriage turned onto the narrow private road, I must take up my life as unwilling mistress of the Fonsell house. We broke through the trees into the clearing and there it was, rising from its neglected lawn. It was not going to be so bad, I told myself, even as I looked at the stucco-coated pillars, the pediment-topped windows that looked like hooded eyes, and that skylight, swelling upward within the railed

47

widow's walk like some noxious bubble about to burst. It was only from the outside that the house was so ugly.

What was more, my aunt would be installed there by now. As we stitched that white wedding gown we had discussed her plans. Rose Murphy would help her close the house, and then move to the Biemeyers, our across-the-street neighbors who had long coveted her services. Then my aunt would take a few of her most cherished possessions to the Fonsell house.

As for Annabelle Clyssom, Jason had assured me that she would not be there. He had hired a new housekeeper, a London-born widow named May Burlow. "She worked for us as an upstairs maid before she left to get married. That was back in palmier days, of course. You may not like her. She's got one of those prune faces. But I think you'll find her efficient."

The carriage stopped before the broad front steps. Jason and the coachman unstrapped my small trunk from the rear luggage platform. As the three of us mounted the steps, the coachman carrying the trunk and Jason his own valise and my small satchel, the front door opened. A woman stood there, wearing a bib apron over a blue cotton shirtwaist and full skirt.

"Hello, Mrs. Burlow."

"Good afternoon, Mr. Jason." Enough of her Cockney accent remained that it almost sounded like "hafternoon." A widow, Jason had said. However long or short her marriage, it could not have been a happy one. Her mouth had the pinched bitterness, and her eyes the lurking, mean little smile, of a woman who had found life, and especially people, a disappointment.

She opened the door wide. Jason said, before the three of us stepped past her, "This is Mrs. Fonsell, Mrs. Burlow."

Her pinched smile widened slightly. "A pleasure to meet you, I'm sure."

In the lower hall Jason paid the coachman. When the door had closed behind him, Jason turned to me, "I suppose you'd like to rest."

"Yes, and freshen up." The train ride from New York had been long, and the coach window sills and seat backs grimy with coal dust.

"I'll bring your trunk up later. Right now I want to see my father." He handed my satchel to the housekeeper. "Please show Mrs. Fonsell to her room."

As I moved after her toward the foot of the stairs, I reflected that however ugly the façade of the house, this staircase was beautiful. Spiraling upward through all three stories, it led the eye to the pale green glow pouring down through the domed skylight.

I asked, "Where is my aunt?"

"She's napping. Older people nap a lot." Glancing back at me over her shoulder, she added with sour relish, "Happens to everybody, in time."

Jason's presentiment had been right. I was not going to like Mrs. Burlow. I asked, as we climbed the stairs, "Where is her room?"

"First floor, towards the back. Right under your room, as a matter of fact. She's got the nicest bedroom in the house. It used to be Mrs. Fonsell's room, Mrs. Ephraim Fonsell, that is."

The dead woman's room. But it was not in that room that she had died. And even if it had been, there was no place in my aunt's stanchly Presbyterian views for superstition.

Near the end of the second floor hall she opened a door. "Mr. Jason told me you'd have this room."

It was pleasant enough, with a four-poster bed of dark wood, and a braided oval rug on the wide-boarded floor, and flowered chintz draperies at the window. She set my satchel on the dressing table. Hand on the doorknob, she asked, "Anything else?"

"Yes. What time will we have dinner?"

Her reply came so promptly that I felt she had been waiting for that question. "Isn't that for you to say? You're the mistress."

So it was to be like that. Because I was young, and the object of village gossip, she hoped to embarrass and intimidate me. I said, trying to speak with my aunt's calm dignity, "You're quite right. Tomorrow we shall sit down and go over all the household schedules. But tonight we will have dinner at whatever hour you have been serving Mr. Fonsell and Miss Haverly and Miss Ruth."

She said, "Six-thirty, ma'am." That "ma'am," I felt, had slipped out in spite of her.

I nodded and said, "Thank you." She closed the door.

Half an hour later, wearing a dark blue woolen dress in place of my skirt and jacket, I emerged from my room. At the stair landing I halted, looking up at the green glow, dimmer now, which poured through the skylight. For the first time I noticed, showing through the glass, the pattern of protective steel mesh on its outer surface. I began to climb. It was still only four o'clock. There would be time to look at the third floor.

Anyone would have known that this floor had been set aside for a domestic staff. The doors were set closer together than on the lower floors. The hall runner was of straw rather than wool. There were signs of neglect, too. Dust lay thick on the banister rail, and the brown plaster walls were cracked and stained.

I looked up at the skylight, and at the heavy collar of wood, painted white, upon which it rested. The paint was discolored and peeling. I thought, suddenly, of the widow's walk surrounding that glass bubble. How absurd! No means had been provided for a widow or anyone else to gain access to that walk. Well, people said that Ephraim Fonsell had designed this house himself. Undoubtedly that widow's walk had been an afterthought. Since such structures had been the fashion forty years ago, he'd had one built atop his own roof.

I heard the sound of footsteps crossing a room somewhere to my left. Mrs. Burlow, undoubtedly. I moved to an open doorway and looked in.

A full-figured woman in a green skirt and tight, green-and-white-checked jacket stood there, bending over a bed which had been stripped to its muslin mattress cover. With one hand, she was stuffing what appeared to be a red woolen scarf into a carpetbag. She turned her handsome face, framed in reddish-brown hair, toward me. With a surge of outrage, I saw that she was Annabelle Clyssom.

She straightened. Before I could demand what she was doing here, she said, smiling slightly, "I came back for some things I'd left."

No doubt. But why had she left them? And why had she come back for them on this particular day? She must have known, if not from Jason himself, then from the account in the *Express*, that we would return today "after a ten-day honeymoon in New York."

I asked, "Did Mrs. Burlow let you in?"

Unlike Mrs. Burlow's, Annabelle's insolence was neither covert nor sly. Bold amusement curved her full mouth, and shone in her brown eyes. "I let myself in, through the back way."

"Then you still have a key?"

"What key? Nobody around here locks doors. Did you and your aunt lock your doors over on Howard Street?"

We had not, nor had any of our neighbors. But somehow I had thought that the doors of this tragedy-haunted house would be locked.

Lifting the carpetbag from the bed, she hefted it in her hand. "Well, it's heavy, but I have only about a mile to

51

walk." She paused. "I'm living in one of those new cottages in Redwood."

I knew then why she had come here today. She wanted to remind me that although I had the title of Mrs. Jason Fonsell, she had Jason. I said, "Yes, Jason told me he was going to make some such arrangement for you."

My calm tone must have shaken her at least momentarily, because her smile wavered, and then broadened. "Do you know something? You've got spunk. Years ago when I'd see you on the street with your aunt, I'd think, 'She's got spunk, that little one.' And you have. Most girls in your spot would have headed for the tall timber. But you figured out a way to stay here, and look people in the eye, and say, 'Prove it!'"

I stiffened. How much had Jason told her? Had he discussed Steven and me with his—his doxy?

She said, as if I had asked the question, "No, Jason didn't tell me you're expecting. But he did tell me that he was marrying you only to get money from your aunt, and you knew it. I didn't have to be a genius to figure out why a girl would be willing to marry a man on those terms."

She moved toward the door. "Well, goodbye." As she walked past me, I caught a whiff of the patchouli which, ever since I was a child, I had associated with the Fonsells' housekeeper. I waited a moment, and then stepped out into the hall in time to see her red-brown head disappear down the narrow rear staircase.

Late afternoon shadows were filling the hall now. I moved through them to a small round window set beside the rear stairwell and looked down. Yes, there was the garden, its lawn brown and its flower beds along the brick walls still holding the frost-blackened stalks of last summer's blooms. As I watched, Annabelle emerged from the back door, moved down the flagstone walk, and pushed open the wooden gate. I watched her move across the clearing toward a break in the trees, evidently the start of a path which would lead her to the North Haven bridge and then along the cove's opposite shore to the point of sparsely settled land known as Redwood. It was not until she disappeared that I realized she had not actually told me whether or not she had a key. Well, it didn't matter. I did not think she would come back. And all I cared about was that, as long as my aunt and I were here, Annabelle did not stir up additional talk by frequenting this house.

My gaze went to the garden's right-hand wall. Yes, there it was, the oak tree branch extending over the wall's coping, the branch which I had noticed during my childhood visit to this house, and which, after the murder, had figured in my nightmares. Had Mrs. Fonsell's slayer really dropped, panther-like, from that branch? Probably not. Probably he had come through that gate. Or—terrible and yet recurring thought—he had come out of this house, slipping from the back door to where an unsuspecting woman stood in the moonlight—

"Yes, that's where it happened."

With a startled cry I turned around and looked into the small gray eyes, the lined face. "Mrs. Burlow! I didn't hear you."

"I've always been light on my feet." Her tone was smug. "But look, let me show you where it happened. See that tree branch sticking over the wall? They found her lying on the ground the next morning, halfway between there and the gate."

Even though I knew the answer, I asked, "Found who?"

"Why, Mrs. Fonsell, of course. Funny thing is, nobody heard her cry out. Whoever did it must have sneaked up behind her and stunned her before she knew what was happening."

Either that, or—the reluctant, inescapable thought again —he had been someone she knew and trusted, someone she might even have welcomed with a smile.

53

I could not resist asking, "Did you work here then?"

"Off and on. I wasn't here the night of the murder, but I used to come in once a week to help Annabelle with heavy cleaning. You see, the Fonsells had had to let all the other full-time help go." She gave her pinched little smile. "I guess Mr. Fonsell had figured that if they could have only one in help, she might as well be good-looking."

I knew it was shameful to stand here gossiping with her, and yet again I could not resist asking a question. "Which Mr. Fonsell?"

"Why, old Mr. Fonsell, of course. Mr. Ephraim. Mr. Jason wasn't much more than a boy then." She chuckled briefly. "I think maybe, after old Mr. Fonsell's wife was killed, Annabelle had hopes that he might marry her. But it didn't turn out like that. Seemed he liked to look at her, but that was all."

She cocked her head to one side. "Didn't I hear Annabelle talking up here a while ago?"

"Yes. She came back for some things she had forgotten." Only Mrs. Burlow's eyes said, "I'll bet." Her voice said, "Anyway, I don't blame Mr. Fonsell for wanting to have a good-looking, friendly face around. People say he's an old probate, but—"

"A probate?" I said, and then realized she must mean reprobate.

"That's what they call him. But I say there can be two sides to that question. Maybe Mrs. Fonsell wasn't all she should be."

That was too much. Neither before nor after her death, as far as I knew, had anyone spoken ill of Ephraim Fonsell's beautiful wife. And in a village as small as ours, where everyone knew and observed everyone else, that must have meant that there was nothing ill to say of her. I asked coldly, "What do you mean?"

Her eyes looked a little taken aback, but her tone was defiant. "Oh, I never heard or saw anything. But the last few weeks before she was killed, there was—oh, I don't know, a kind of glow about her. I'd come over to help clean house, and from the look of her I got the feeling she wasn't even *in* this house. She was a way off in some sort of place that nobody knew anything about."

Had Julia Fonsell been unusually happy in the weeks before her death? Or was that "glow" only the envious imagination of a woman who probably had never glowed in her life?

She said, almost as if she had caught a fragment of my thought, "Well, she's been dead ten years now, almost, so what good did it do her, whatever she was so happy about?"

Whereas May Burlow was alive. Sly, sour, and corroded with envy, but alive.

I wanted to end this conversation. But first I had to try to restore the proper distance between us. "Since you spoke of heavy cleaning a moment ago, couldn't a little of it be done on this floor?" I trailed my fingers along the window sill and then held out my hand to her. Even in the gathering dark, the dust on my fingers was visible.

Her voice became shrilly defensive. "That's not fair, Mrs. Fonsell. I'm only one person. Miss Ruth is supposed to help me, but she doesn't, not much. And this is a big house."

It certainly was. I began to feel ashamed of myself. What right did I have to condemn her, when I had no idea of just how bleak her life had been? As for her gossiping, I had listened, hadn't I?

I said, "I'll help you." I would, too, as long as I could. And come early spring, I would do whatever I was able to in the neglected garden. My reason would be not just to make myself useful. I once had heard Dr. Cantrell remark that there would be more healthy children if, in the months before their birth, their mothers had remained active. "Instead they loll around reading Longfellow and Sir Walter Scott, in the ridiculous delusion that they're endowing their offspring with artistic tendencies."

"Well," I said, turning away, "I must see if my aunt is awake."

As I approached her first floor room I saw a thread of light under her door. I tapped lightly. Almost immediately the door opened. "Oh, Irene! I was just coming to look for you."

Feeling a surprised relief, I gathered her close and, although I knew she did not approve of kissing, planted a kiss on her cheek. I had feared to find her in worse health than when I had left. Instead she appeared improved. Some of the anxious lines had smoothed out of her face, and she had even gained a little weight.

I said, holding her at arm's length, "You look wonderful."

"I am better. But I want to hear about you. Come over by the fire."

It was not until we were seated in slipper chairs flanking a small, marble-manteled fireplace that I noticed, affixed to the wall behind her, the etched glass globe of a gas jet. "Why, I didn't know this house had gas!"

Illuminating gas had been introduced into Sag Harbor in 1859, when I was still a small child. But my aunt, disapproving of such frills, had clung to her oil lamps.

She smiled. "I must admit it's more convenient. No wicks to trim, no chimneys to clean. But tell me, child, how are you?"

"I'm fine. And I enjoyed New York." I told her a little of the theatrical performances I had seen, and the shops I had visited.

She asked, in a constrained voice, "And Jason?"

I shrugged. "We had dinner together each evening. Otherwise I seldom saw him. I gather he was attending to business matters." I paused, again wondering at Jason's grim, single-minded ambition. "But tell me, what has it been like—"

"To stay in this house? I haven't minded. Perhaps it was

56

because I so dreaded coming here. Now I can tell you how much I dreaded it. By contrast, I suppose, the reality has been quite pleasant."

"But Jason's father—"

"He's lived a wicked and wasteful life, Irene, and he shows no sign of repentance. But he's been very pleasant to me. No fine Christian gentleman could have been nicer."

Fine Christian gentleman. I thought of him at that ceremony in the parsonage ten days before—bushy-browed, red-faced, and obviously harboring a monumental thirst.

"He even refrains from drinking in my presence."

I said, impressed, "That is remarkable."

"I hope it improves his health. The poor man's stomach must be in a dreadful state."

I leaned forward to poke the coal fire that glowed in the grate. Replacing the poker in its brass stand, I asked, "And Ruth?"

"She's a strange girl, but she's been polite to me. Distant, but polite." She hesitated. "I'm sure Dr. Cantrell would not have told me this if he hadn't known you and I were to move into this house. Perhaps I had better tell you so that you will understand Ruth better."

A runaway horse, it seemed, had upset a buggy in which four-year-old Ruth and a nursemaid were riding. Thrown to the roadside, Ruth had struck her head against a fence post. "I remember the incident, but you wouldn't. You were only a toddler then. Anyway, Dr. Cantrell believes she suffered brain damage. Until that time she had been a normal child. But after that she cried frequently, and if anyone crossed her she went into a screaming rage. Then, when she was nine or ten, she changed again. She became well-behaved and quiet, too quiet."

What had become, I wondered, of the easily infuriated Ruth who had emerged after the accident? Had she lurked beneath the surface of the Ruth who had sat in the Misses

57

Pride's classes, composed and meticulously neat? Did she still lurk there? Perhaps. Perhaps without knowing it, others sensed the sobbing, enraged, uncontrollable Ruth beneath the serene exterior. Perhaps that was why she'd had no friends while she was growing up, and had no suitors now.

I said, into the silence, "Has Dr. Cantrell been here?"

"Yes, to see me."

"Is he Mr. Fonsell's doctor?"

"He once was, about fifteen years ago. But Mr. Fonsell wouldn't obey orders. And you know how Dr. Cantrell is. He'll take only so much nonsense. Finally he told Mr. Fonsell he was washing his hands of him. Since then he's been treated by Dr. Ronsard."

I had heard of Paul Ronsard, a Southampton doctor who'd had notable success in treating sufferers from heart and circulatory ailments. In fact, Dr. Cantrell had told me that if my aunt's condition worsened he would turn to Dr. Ronsard for advice.

My aunt said, "You haven't told me what you think of this room."

Intent upon our talk, I had not really looked at my surroundings, but now I rose and wandered about the big room, illuminated by the mingled glow of gaslight and dancing firelight. I could well believe it was the best bedroom in the house. The mahogany four-poster had a dark blue velvet canopy that matched the bedspread and the draperies at a pair of French doors. An eight-foot-high mahogany wardrobe, with elaborately carved doors, stood against one wall. The carpet appeared to be an Aubusson. I recognized objects she had brought from the Howard Street house. The big calf-bound Bible on the stand beside her bed. Her silver-backed comb and brush set on the dresser, and beside it the music box which had so delighted me as a child. When you lifted the lid, the box played "O Christmas Tree." The red lacquer chest my Grandfather Haverly had brought back from China stood near the fireplace, and above the mantel hung the oval-framed photograph of my father.

As I looked at it, my aunt said, "I hung it there only temporarily. It belongs in your room, of course."

"No, you keep it. I have his miniature." I sat down again in the slipper chair. "Did they tell you—"

I broke off. She said, "That this was once Mrs. Fonsell's room? Of course. The housekeeper lost no time in telling me. I hope you realize that I am far too sensible to mind. She's dead, poor woman. Let us hope that she is in Heaven. But in any event, she doesn't linger in this room."

She hesitated, and then went on, "About the housekeeper. You've met her, of course."

I nodded.

"It would be best to keep your distance with Mrs. Burlow. She is an unhappy woman, and unhappy people often feel a need to disparage others. Be fair to her, of course. But remember that you are mistress here."

I was sure then that Mrs. Burlow had tried to talk about the Fonsells to my aunt. Feeling abashed, I was equally sure that my aunt, unlike me, had refused to listen.

She said, "And since you are the mistress, shouldn't you go into the dining room now and look over the table setting?"

"Doesn't Mrs. Burlow set it properly?"

"She does. But I think you should verify that for yourself."

My aunt was right. By taking over the household reins visibly and firmly right at the start, I would not only establish the proper relationship with Mrs. Burlow, I would also be in a better position to cope with any future crises.

I said, rising, "Then I'll see you at dinner."

Emerging into the hall, I saw that someone had lit sconce wall lights which I had not even noticed before. Through that soft glow, I started toward the front of the house. Then

I stopped short, my heart pounding with incredulous joy. I placed one hand against the wall for support.

Back turned to me, a man was approaching the front door, a tall, slender man whose blond hair gleamed in the gaslight.

Chapter 8

STEVEN!

I don't think that I said the name aloud, but I must have made some sound, because the man turned toward me.

He was not Steven. His face, wearing a puzzled half smile, was older than Steven's, and his eyes were gray rather than blue.

I said, "I beg your pardon. I thought you were someone else." My heart still pounded so hard that I was afraid to take my hand from the wall.

He said pleasantly, "You must be Mrs. Jason Fonsell."

I nodded. Others had called me Mrs. Fonsell—the desk clerk in New York, the waiter who had brought breakfast to my room, and Mrs. Burlow today. But to me the words still sounded grotesque.

He said, "I'm Paul Ronsard, Dr. Ronsard."

I had myself under control now. As I moved toward him I noticed for the first time that he carried a black leather medical bag in his right hand. Transferring it to his left, he grasped the hand I extended. "I've heard of you," I said. "Dr. Cantrell speaks highly of you."

"That's good to know. I think highly of Dr. Cantrell." There were gray streaks in his blond hair, I saw now. To have achieved his present status in the medical profession, he could not have been younger than forty. But even from close up he looked younger, as thin, fair-complexioned men often do. He added, "Is Dr. Cantrell your doctor?"

"Mine and my aunt's. I suppose you have been seeing my father-in-law."

"Yes. I've come here each Wednesday afternoon for the last five years, ever since his condition worsened. With almost any other patient, I would have insisted that he keep on coming to my office. But I was afraid that if I tried that with Ephraim Fonsell he would refuse, and thus probably have no medical attention at all."

"How did you find him today?"

Dr. Ronsard laughed. "He's incredible. When I examined him fifteen years ago—he was one of my first patients—I told him that if he went on guzzling at that rate he wouldn't live out the year. He's gone on guzzling. And living."

I said, still shaken by his resemblance to Steven, "I thought from your name that you were French. You don't look it."

"I had a French great-grandfather. Otherwise my ancestry is English and Danish."

A door closed down the hall. I turned to see Jason moving toward us. He said, "So you two have met." The appraising look he gave me told me that he was aware of Dr. Ronsard's resemblance to Steven, and wondered how I had reacted to it.

I said evenly, "We introduced ourselves."

Jason laid his hand on the other man's arm. "I'll see you out to your surrey, Doctor. I want to ask you about my father."

"All right." He smiled at me. "Good night, Mrs. Fonsell."

When the door had closed behind the two men, I walked through the archway into the room where that long-ago birthday party had been held. Yes, Julia Fonsell's portrait still hung above the fireplace.

I saw that Mrs. Burlow, as if to rebuke me with her competence, had set the table not only correctly but beautifully, with a damask cloth, heavy flat sterling, and Spode china which I suspected—correctly, as it turned out—was not used every day. Glancing at the sideboard, I saw that it held tall crystal decanters, filled almost to their stoppers, and hung with engraved silver tags which identified them as sherry, port, and brandy.

I turned my attention to Julia Fonsell's portrait. How beautiful her painted image was, with its violet eyes, and the silver-blond hair curling around her oval face. I knew the artist had not lied. When I was eight or nine I used to feel awed by the sight of her, riding down Main Street in an open carriage, and flanked by her two handsome blond children.

I continued to study the portrait, noticing details which had escaped me when, as a ten-year-old, I had last been in this room. I saw how gracefully she sat in a dark red wing chair, her narrow hands folded in her lap. I noticed how her simple gown of black velvet made an excellent foil for her slender bare arms, and for the oval pendant of white jade suspended from the thin gold chain around her neck. It was an unusual stone, framed in tiny rubies, and with a lotus bud carved in its center.

Somewhere, not too long ago, I had seen someone else wearing that pendant. Who was it? Ruth Fonsell, no doubt. Had she worn it the day Jason and I were married? No, not then. It was on some previous occasion.

I returned my gaze to Julia Fonsell's face. And then I saw something else which I had been too young to observe during that birthday party. Although the woman in the portrait smiled, her violet eyes held a sad, almost haunted look.

A silken rustle. I turned. Ruth was moving toward me. She wore a low-cut dress of light green silk, far too formal for a family dinner. But perhaps she had put it on in honor of the homecoming of her brother and her new sister-in-law. I said, "Why, hello."

She smiled at me. "Hello, Irene."

I waited for her to say, "Welcome home." Instead, still smiling faintly, she looked down at a table setting and moved its knife a fraction of an inch toward the plate and then back again.

I said brightly, "New York was very interesting. Have you ever been there?"

"No."

"You should go someday. You'd like it."

"No, I wouldn't. I like being in this house."

Silence settled down. Then I said, "I was looking at your mother's portrait. She was so lovely. And so like you."

"She was shorter than me."

Conversations with Ruth were like that. Her answers made sense. And yet they were often so unexpected that you yourself had no reply. It was like bouncing a ball and having it hit some hidden protuberance in the sidewalk, so that it angled away from your waiting hand.

I tried again. "That black dress set off her blondness so beautifully. And that pendant is lovely. You must enjoy wearing it."

"No."

"You mean you don't like it?"

"I've never worn it. I don't even know where it is."

Her tone was so indifferent that we might have been discussing a bit of nickel-a-yard ribbon, rather than a valuable and perhaps unique piece of jewelry. "But I'm sure I've seen someone wearing it. And it must have been you."

"No."

Baffled, I descended to triteness. "You must miss her very much."

She looked up at the painting. "Things were different after she died. I was the lady of the house. My father said so. And even though I was only twelve, Annabelle"—her gaze slid to me, and then away—"would consult me about things."

I could imagine Annabelle, poker-faced, consulting the

64

child about menus, say, and then serving exactly what she pleased.

"And after Mother was dead, I sat in her place at the table."

The place where I would sit. "Ruth, I hope you don't resent my being here."

Not answering, she smiled at me.

"I mean, I hope we'll be friends."

"We've always been friends. We went to school together, didn't we?"

Not attempting a reply, I said, "I've been up on the third floor. It was dusty there. I'd better freshen up before dinner."

Chapter 9

WE TALKED BUSINESS almost exclusively at dinner that night. At least Jason and his father and my aunt talked business. I sat almost as silent as Ruth, eating my roast lamb and whipped potatoes and string beans.

Jason did most of the talking. And in forty minutes I learned more about Fonsell and Haverly than I had in all ten of those uncomfortable dinners at our New York hotel. He had, it seemed, made arrangements with a New Jersey refinery to process his imported raw sugar. Later, of course, he would build his own refinery on "that lot I bought on Bay Street." (When had he bought it? Before our marriage, probably. Which meant that either my aunt had made funds available to him even then, or had guaranteed repayment of a bank loan. In either case, he had never mentioned the matter to me.) He had also inspected a ten-year-old brig at a Brooklyn shipyard. Its price was fairly reasonable, but it needed extensive repairs.

"The Brooklyn yard gave me an estimate for the job. I telegraphed the boat works here in Sag Harbor, giving the details of what would be required, and asking for a rough estimate. The figure they sent back was a little higher. I don't know what to do." He looked at my aunt. "What do you think, Miss Haverly?"

"Have the local yard do it," she said promptly. "Sound neighborliness is sound business. Later you'll find that local people with something to ship to the Caribbean will turn

66

to you, not some New York line who might offer a little better price."

I began to see how it was that my aunt, even with her thoughts fixed firmly on the next world, had managed to do so well with Grandfather Haverly's money in this one.

"You're right, Miss Haverly," Ephraim Fonsell said, and Jason nodded a thoughtful agreement.

It was not until the apple shortcake was served that I realized that Ephraim Fonsell had not once visited the sideboard. Nor had he, after any of Mrs. Burlow's appearances through the green baize pantry door, asked her to bring him a decanter. My aunt, at least at mealtimes, had turned my father-in-law into an abstainer.

When Mrs. Burlow had taken the dessert plates away, Jason pushed back his chair and said, "If you'll excuse me, I won't have coffee. I've got paper work up in my room. And I'd better go back to New York tomorrow, and see if I can get a lower price on that brig."

I watched him walk toward the hall. Which room, I wondered, was his?

With appalling suddenness, I was seized by an impulse to break into both laughter and tears. Laughter, because I did not know which room was occupied by the man I had married. And tears because I should not even be in this house. Steven and I should be in our own little house, delighting in the sight of each other across a small table, and exchanging little jokes about the baby. I swallowed hard and, beneath the table, gripped my hands together.

"Irene." From under gray-black brows, Ephraim Fonsell was watching me. "Don't you think it's time we got acquainted? Why don't you come see me in about half an hour? I'll be in the den. Ruth will show you where it is."

"All right." In my present mood, I did not want to inflict myself upon my aunt. Nor did I want to be alone the rest of the evening.

About forty minutes later, Ruth walked with me to a door near the end of the first floor hall. I knocked. When Ephraim's voice answered, Ruth nodded to me, that odd little smile hovering on her lips, and turned away.

I found him seated in a black leather wing chair, with the dancing light from a coal fire in the grate making his red face even redder. "Have a chair," he said. "Excuse me for not getting up. I'm an old man, and a sick one."

No wonder, I thought, as I sat down in the wing chair on the opposite side of the small fireplace. Plainly he was making up for time lost at dinner. On the small rosewood liquor cabinet beside him sat a bottle and a half-full glass of brandy.

"Would you like some Madeira? A lady's drink, mild and sweet. Or are you temperance, like your aunt?"

"Not strictly." At two parties during the previous Christmas season I had taken a glass of punch. And in New York Jason had ordered wine to accompany those strained, mostly silent dinners of ours. "But I don't care for anything now, thank you."

He did not urge me. Instead he took a long swallow of brandy and then said, "Your aunt is a remarkable woman, a really good woman. I don't mean just chaste. Country's full of chaste women." He sounded as if he found the fact deplorable. "I mean *good*.

"But I didn't call you in here to talk about your aunt. I want to talk about you." His dark eyes, surprisingly bright, regarded me from under shaggy brows. "You nearly went to pieces at dinner tonight. We can't have that. Not your business to go on grieving and regretting, no matter what fools you and Steven were."

His voice roughened as he said his son's name, and that surprised me. I don't know why. No matter what he was, there was no reason to assume that he was incapable of grief. "You know what your business is now, don't you?"

"I think so."

"Your business is to give me a healthy grandson."

His grandson. The drunken old egotist. I said stiffly, "I have every hope that my child, mine and—" My throat closed up.

Again I was aware of his keen gaze. "Better not to talk about him now. Plenty of time for that later on. All I'll say now is that I guess it's true that often the good die young." He tipped more brandy into his glass. "It's my sort that make old bones."

Not really wanting to know, only wanting to distract myself, I asked, "Why do you drink so much, when your doctor—"

"Damn young fool."

I had liked Paul Ronsard. "If you think he's a fool, why do you keep him as your doctor?"

"Because he's the only one who will put up with me. And I'll bet he wouldn't, if he had a wife and children to support. He'd stay in his Southampton office, raking in the money. He wouldn't trot over here once a week to visit an old hulk like me."

After a moment I said, "When I first saw Dr. Ronsard tonight, I thought—" Again my throat closed up.

"I know. He's tall and blond, like Steven. But don't let that give you any ideas. When Paul first came to eastern Long Island, fresh out of an Ohio medical school, Steven was already three years old, and Ruth a year older."

I said, after several seconds of silent indignation, "Why, it never occurred to me that—"

"No, I suppose it didn't. I suppose it has to some people, though. But Ruth and Steven were just lucky enough to inherit their mother's looks. Jason is the only one of my children to get stuck with mine." He filled his glass. "You didn't want to come to this house, did you?"

"No."

"Why? Because you think I killed Julia?"

The question came so suddenly that I could only look at him, sitting there with his bright old eyes reflecting the flames. At last I managed to say, "Some people—"

"They're damn fools. Just because I've always been a carouser, they think I could be a murderer too. The two things have got nothing to do with each other. Besides, I had no reason. Julia and I got along fine. True, she was a cold woman, but that kind make the best mothers."

A cold woman. I remembered Mrs. Burlow's spiteful words, up there on the darkening third floor. "There was this kind of glow about her." I hadn't believed Mrs. Burlow then, and I believed her less now.

"Julia fitted this house. She was the kind of wife I had in mind when I built it, back in 1833."

I could understand that. To Ephraim, who had built it, this house must appear elegant and impressive, and he had wanted to match it with an elegant and beautiful woman. But what I couldn't understand was why she had married him. Even granting that she was the sort of woman who regards a husband mainly as a means of getting children, why had she chosen this particular husband, a coarse-grained man twice her age?

"Not that I was ready to get married back in 1833. I was only twenty-nine then. But I was rich. The captain's share of two whaling voyages had made me rich. People these days forget how young the masters of those whalers were. Lots of us were under thirty. Whaling was a young man's work, work you might get killed at. When you tied into a whale you never knew who was going to win out. Why, I remember once when we put two whaleboats over the side, me in one and my first mate in the other—"

As he went on talking, he made me see it. The harpooned whale, fighting for her life, turning in water stained by her own blood to smash the first mate's fragile boat with her tail. "My boat managed to pick up several of the men in the

water, but two of them—stunned by that blow, I guess—
went under, and the water was so dark with blood that nobody could see where to dive in after them. As for the mate,
the whale rushed at him, caught him in her mouth, and
sounded. Whether she died down there, with the mate still
in her mouth, I don't know. We waited two hours, and then
sailed."

I asked slowly, "Was it worth all that, the danger, the
death?"

"Worth it! Good lord, girl. You bet it was, and not just
for the money. Why, before I was thirty, I'd been all over
the world. South America, Australia, Fiji Islands, the Arctic,
San Francisco—"

Jason's mother, I had heard, had come from San Francisco.

"I even had the chance to be king of a cannibal island.
Real cannibals, you understand, but only when they were
holding religious ceremonies. Weekdays, so to speak, they
ate like anybody else, fish and wild pig and breadfruit. Anyway, this king wanted to adopt me and marry me to his
daughter. That daughter! She must have weighed three hundred pounds. Funny she was so fat, when lots of the other
girls on that island— But maybe I'd better not talk about
that."

I was surprised to feel a smile tugging at the corners of
my mouth. "Maybe you'd better not."

"Well, anyway, the best port of all was home port. Not
that I had any family waiting for me."

I nodded. From Steven I had learned that Ephraim's father, a privateersman during the 1812 War, had been lost
at sea when Ephraim was nine. While he was still in his
teens, his mother had died.

"Just the same, it was great to sail through Plum Gut
with the holds filled with sperm oil, and catch the first sight
of that Old Whalers' Church steeple."

As he talked on, I could picture how our now-quiet village must have seemed to returning whalemen in the exhilarating 1830s and 1840s. At the cry of "Ship in the bay!" everyone in town who wasn't too old or too young or too sick would rush down to Long Wharf. Once the vessel was tied up, it meant money for the whole village. Riggers and carpenters and calkers would swarm over the weather-battered vessel, preparing it for its next voyage. Village clerks would race from the ship to warehouses and shops and then back again, taking and filling orders for provisions.

In the meantime, whalemen of almost every nationality and color—Fijians, Malays, Portuguese, Shinnecock Indians, and native-born white Long Islanders—thronged Main Street, reeling in and out of grog shops, displaying bits of whalebone and wood they had carved during long months at sea, and tossing coins to the hero-worshipping small boys who trooped after them, as if after so many drunken Pied Pipers. And at night down at Lambs Corner, near the southern end of the village, the red light would burn until dawn, and the sound of revelry would sometimes swell loud enough to trouble the sleep of respectable folk.

"Always been lots of respectable folks at this end of Long Island. Damned hypocrites, some of them, like the ones who sold cattle to the enemy fleet back in 1812. But there have always been really good people here too, like the Haverlys, and that kind I had respect for. Most whalemen did. When the Presbyterian Church was built, whalemen chipped in. I've never been in the damned—never been in that church in my life, but Fonsell money went into it."

Steven had come to church, though. For a moment I was sixteen again, not quite daring to look back at him, but turning my head so that I could feel his gaze upon my cheek.

"All over," Ephraim said. "Those days will never come again, not anywhere on earth."

I nodded. Although the last Sag Harbor whaler, the *Myra*, had been broken up in Barbados and sold for scrap only two years before, in 1871, the great whaling days had ended before I was born. For one thing, the whales themselves, diminished in number by the wide-ranging slaughter, had retreated to the ice-bound latitudes near the poles. For another, the opening of the Pennsylvania oil fields had reduced the need for whale oil, and at the same time attracted workmen who otherwise might have manned and serviced the whaling fleet. But even before the drilling of the first Pennsylvania oil well, the discovery of gold in California had wreaked disaster upon the whaling industry. Men had left Long Island in such numbers—packed in ships sailing around the Horn, or making their way overland by any means available—that for a time, my aunt had told me, Sag Harbor people had called California "Western Long Island." And the crews of the few whalers that did sail from Long Wharf jumped ship at the first port of call, and took passage on San Francisco-bound vessels.

"But I was finished even before that," Ephraim said. "Funny thing, the year that was the best for other Sag Harbor whalemen was the worst for me. Cargo worth almost a million was unloaded here in 1847, but I didn't make a cent. Instead, I lost a lot of money. My own ship didn't bring back enough sperm oil to pay for the hardtack and bully beef I'd bought before I left. Another ship in which I had a half interest had no better luck. And a third one I'd invested in disappeared somewhere off the Fiji Islands."

And so, in 1849, hoping to recoup his losses, he had taken passage aboard a California-bound schooner.

"The last time I'd been in California was in 1846, when I'd had to put in there for repairs after a bad storm off Hawaii. That was when I met Jason's mother. She was the daughter of a tavern keeper who rented out rooms on the second floor." He looked at me sternly from under those bristly brows. "And no matter what folks think, Marie was no trollop. She was just twenty then, and already a widow.

Her husband, a carpenter named Jackson, had been killed in a fall from a rooftree. I know women, and I know that until I came along there'd been no other man in her life except her husband.

"I didn't hear from her after I left. She didn't know how to read or write, and I guess she was too shy to ask anyone to write a letter for her. Or maybe the idea never occurred to her. Anyway, when I went out there again in 1849, I found she had this two-year-old. I knew he was my son. Spitting image of me. And so when I was ready to leave—I hadn't found any gold to speak of, any more than other Long Island men did—I told her she could come with me. I'd see to it that she was always provided for, and I'd acknowledge Jason as my son and raise him that way. So I brought her to this house."

Only to turn her out a few years later. I wondered what she thought of it all, that illiterate woman living out her life alone in a Long Island hamlet three thousand miles from where she had grown up. Did Ephraim ever visit her? Did her son?

But of course I could not ask those questions. Besides, the heat of the room, and the brandy fumes, and the lateness of the hour had combined to weight my eyelids. He said, "Getting sleepy? Better run along. We'll have plenty of chances to talk."

I bade him good night. A few minutes later in my room, as I was about to take the tortoise-shell pins from my hair, someone knocked. I opened the door and saw Jason standing there.

He said, "I came to say goodbye, since you may not be up by the time I leave in the morning."

I nodded. "Have a good trip."

"How did you and my father get along?"

"Well enough."

"What did you talk about?"

"Oh, he reminisced about whaling."

Jason waited. Obviously he hoped I would say more. Enjoying his frustration, I remained silent. At last he said, "Well, good night," and turned away.

What did he fear we had discussed? His dead stepmother? His relations with Annabelle Clyssom?

In that instant, I realized where I had seen the white jade pendant of the portrait downstairs. I remembered how, one Sunday afternoon two summers before, I had seen Jason's mistress descend from the train at Sag Harbor depot. In a jacket and skirt of emerald-green silk rep, and with a green-plumed black velvet toque covering most of her red-brown hair, she had looked like almost anything but a housekeeper. And on her full bosom, suspended by a gold chain around her neck, had rested a white jade pendant encircled by small red stones.

I called involuntarily, "Jason!"

He turned and moved toward me. "Yes?"

Embarrassed now, and wishing I hadn't called him back, I said, "I was wondering about the jade pendant, the one your stepmother wore for her portrait."

His eyes were both puzzled and wary. "What about it?"

"I—well, I once saw Annabelle Clyssom wearing it."

His tone was cold. "I'm sure you're mistaken."

"But I'm not! It was two summers ago. Probably you were at sea then. But she was getting off the train—she must have been to New York, from the way she was dressed —and she was wearing the pendant. Not," I added lamely, "that it's any of my business."

"You're quite right. It's none of your business. Probably you were mistaken. But if by any chance she does have it, I'm sure she didn't steal it, if that's what you're thinking. My stepmother must have given it to her."

That seemed unlikely. Why should Julia Fonsell have given to her housekeeper a valuable ornament, especially one she was so fond of that she had worn it for her portrait? Perhaps she had, though. Or perhaps she had never given it to anyone. Perhaps she had been wearing it the night that, in the walled garden of this house, someone had struck her down, so suddenly that she could not even cry out . . .

I brought my thoughts up short. As Jason and I had agreed, what had become of the pendant was none of my business. Nor was anything that had happened in this house before I entered it. For as long as I stayed here, it would be well to remember that, if only so that I might remain as tranquil as possible.

"Well, good night," I said, and closed my door.

A few seconds later, I heard another door open and then close. To judge from the sound, it was across the hall and near the front of the house. So now, I reflected wryly, I knew where my husband's room was.

Chapter 10

JASON WAS GONE by the time I came downstairs the next morning. Nor did I see much of him during the following months. Even when he was at home, business matters—as well, no doubt, as visits to Annabelle's cottage among the red cedars and tar pines of Redwood—kept him away from the house for many hours each day and evening.

I was too busy to take much notice of either his presence or his absence. As Mrs. Burlow had said, this was indeed a large house. Although she continued to cook and serve, I took over most of the other housework. Whether out of a desire to help, or a fear that she might be excluded from household management entirely, Ruth assigned herself certain tasks, such as waxing furniture and polishing the ornate flat silver we used for Sunday dinners and on Wednesday nights, when Dr. Ronsard dined with us.

I was the one who invited him the first time. He had said promptly, "I'd be delighted. Just wait until I drive my surrey around to the carriage house." At dinner he proved to be such an enjoyable guest—countering my father-in-law's attacks on "damn fool doctors" with an unruffled smile, discussing Long Island history with my aunt, and complimenting Mrs. Burlow on her ham with raisin sauce—that I was not surprised when, at the end of the evening, Ephraim said, "If you insist on coming over here every Wednesday, you might as well stay for dinner from now on."

"Thank you very much," Paul Ronsard said. "I'll do that."

All that late fall and winter I attended church with Aunt

Elizabeth. Supported by her presence, I found that I could meet the congregation's gaze—in some cases anxiously sympathetic, in others scandalized or merely curious—with a composure designed to say, in Annabelle Clyssom's phrase, "Prove it."

Several times during the twice-weekly shopping trips Aunt Elizabeth and I made to Main Street, I saw Annabelle. She never spoke to me, just nodded with an amused but not unfriendly look in her brown eyes. I was sure that Jason would never have married her. That seemed rather a pity. They were a good match, both of them apparently indifferent to the opinions of others, and single-minded in pursuit of whatever they wanted.

Ruth never accompanied Aunt Elizabeth and me on shopping trips, nor to church. One gray December afternoon, as she and I sat at the pine table in the big kitchen, polishing a pair of silver candelabra, I asked, "Ruth, why is it you almost never leave this house?"

She drew a sponge along a groove in the candelabra's base. "I like it here."

"Well, of course. It's your home. But I should think you would also like to get out and see people."

"I've never liked being out of this house. I even hated going to that school in Bridgehampton. It was better than getting sent away to a boarding school in Connecticut, the way I almost was. Still, I hated the academy."

I said, astonished, "But Ruth! You were the star pupil." True, her grades in arithmetic, history, and composition had been poor. But to the Misses Pride those subjects had been of secondary importance. Ruth excelled in the really essential parts of the curriculum, such as deportment, penmanship, and needlework.

"Just the same, I hated it."

After a moment's hesitation, I said, "But what about when you marry? Your husband may not want to live here."

"I don't want to marry. And no one wants to marry me."

"Perhaps someone would, if you offered a little encouragement. I can tell that Dr. Ronsard admires your looks."

Ruth shrugged. "You're the one he likes."

I felt a little glow of pleasure. From the warmth in Paul Ronsard's gray eyes when he smiled at me, I knew he did like me. I said wryly, "But I'm scarcely eligible."

"Neither am I, unless I want to be."

"Ruth, I can understand your loving your home." That was not true, of course. I would never understand her loving this house where her mother had been battered to death. "But with you it seems to be an obsession."

"I don't care what you call it. I don't even like being out of doors." That seemed to be the case. Sometimes she would sit with her embroidery in one of the rattan porch chairs, but she seldom went willingly even as far as the stable and carriage house at the rear of the Fonsell property, let alone as far as the cove, or across the bridge to Main Street. "I don't feel safe outside this house."

"Ruth! Why?"

The sponge still in her hand, she looked across the table at me. The pupils of her blue eyes, I saw with a sense of shock, had contracted to tiny black dots.

"Something terrible happened to me outdoors." Her voice had taken on the hushed, faraway tone of a frightened child's. "I was lying there under the sky, and my head hurt terribly, and I knew that something awful had happened to me. Then someone picked me up and carried me, and that hurt even more. But after a while I woke up with a ceiling over me. I still hurt, and I still knew the awful thing had happened. But I felt it wouldn't matter too much if I didn't have to go out of this house."

"You remember that accident? Why, you were only four."

"I remember it."

Apparently she did. And perhaps as she had lain there,

shrieking with pain under the vast and terrible sky, she had somehow known that her small brain had suffered irrevocable damage, ending her hope of a normal life almost before her life had begun. I said inadequately, "Ruth, I'm so sorry."

She set to work with the sponge. "That's all right." Her little smile was back in place. "I don't think of it very often."

We worked in silence until Mrs. Burlow came into the kitchen, looked sourly at the gleaming candelabra and tarnish-blackened sponges, and asked how a person could be expected to make dinner with that mess on the table.

Ten days later, in time for Christmas, Jason returned from New York. The occasion was marked, not only by the traditional turkey, but by the first clash between Jason and me since that morning when we settled our living arrangements.

Ephraim had invited Paul Ronsard for Christmas dinner which, in deference to the routine Ephraim was supposed to follow, was served at the usual dinner hour of six-thirty. After Mrs. Burlow had brought in the plum pudding, Dr. Ronsard said, "Jason, your father tells me you've signed a contract with a New Jersey sugar refinery."

Even though Jason did not glance at Ephraim, I sensed he was annoyed that his father had discussed his business affairs. "Yes."

"I'd thought you were just going to import raw sugar, not refine it and market it." When Jason didn't reply, Paul Ronsard went on, "I admire your enterprise. But don't you think you're taking on quite a lot all at once?"

"I intend to take on even more. Before long I'll be refining my own sugar, here in Sag Harbor."

Paul Ronsard smiled. "Well, as a medical man, I feel duty-bound to warn you that overactive businessmen have a high mortality rate."

Jason also smiled. "As a medical man, you should feel it your duty to advise your patients. I'm not one of them."

After a moment Paul said lightly, "And a good thing, too. I don't think you'd follow my orders any more than your father does."

Dr. Ronsard left soon after dinner. By nine-thirty, my aunt had gone to bed. A few minutes later I said good night, and went into the hall. Hearing swift footsteps behind me, I turned.

Jason said, "Why was Ronsard here? Christmas is supposed to be a family occasion."

I said coolly, "Dr. Ronsard has no relatives nearer than Ohio. Besides, I didn't invite him. Your father did."

He didn't answer that. "I understand he's been staying for dinner each Wednesday night."

"At your father's standing invitation. Now that you're here so seldom, I think he likes having another younger man at his table. Do you object? If so, talk to him about it."

"Ronsard wouldn't accept the invitations if my father was the only one who wanted him here."

"That's right. My aunt and Ruth and I enjoy his company, too. In fact, I think there's a chance he and Ruth will become interested in each other."

Jason laughed. "Irene, your trouble is that you think you can play foxy tricks on a fox. If Ronsard stays Wednesday nights because he's interested in something besides conversation and home cooking, that something isn't Ruth."

"I'm not playing foxy tricks!" Aware that Ephraim and Ruth might hear, I lowered my voice. "But even if I were, under the terms of our agreement you'd have no right to object, would you?"

"None whatever." His tone was as cool as mine. "I just don't want you to think I'm such a fool as not to see which way the wind blows."

"Which way the—!" I got my voice under control. "What you're implying is as stupid as it is insulting. In my present circumstances, I can have concern for only two persons—my

81

aunt, and the child I am going to have. If you don't want Dr. Ronsard staying for dinner," I said, as I turned toward the stairs, "then tell your father so."

Jason was gone the next day. Evidently he said nothing to his father about those Wednesday night dinners before he left, because Dr. Ronsard continued to sit at our table once a week, good-naturedly countering Ephraim's rough banter, talking about books and gardening and local politics, and sometimes bringing a look of interest even to Ruth's aloofly smiling face.

In February, as was proper, I discontinued church attendance and my shopping trips across the bridge. But from inclination as well as because of Dr. Cantrell's advice, I took a daily walk through the woods down to the cove whenever the weather permitted. When winter relaxed into a mild, early spring, I often carried a carpet-covered folding stool down to the sand and sat there for an hour or so.

One bright April morning I found that someone had arrived before me. He stood there at an easel planted near the water's edge, a thin, dark-bearded man of forty-odd. We exchanged nods. As I passed him, intending to seek a spot farther along the shore, I noticed the wooden carrying case that stood on the sand near his feet. On it, painted in black letters, was the name John R. Solum.

I halted. "Why, you're the man who painted Mrs. Fonsell's portrait." I felt a stir of excitement. Here was someone who had known that lovely and tragically fated woman—strange to think that she was my child's grandmother—near the end of her life. John Solum had completed his portrait of her only weeks before her death.

He turned his thin, high-cheekboned face toward me. "Mrs. Ephraim Fonsell? Yes, I painted her." He returned his gaze to his easel-propped canvas and made a brush stroke.

I looked at the canvas. In the right foreground he had painted the rotting planks of the *Apollo* and the *Franklin*, two sloops that had sunk years ago west of Long Wharf, and whose remains were still visible at low tide. Beyond was the sparkling expanse of the bay with Shelter Island in the left background, the unfurling leaves of its deciduous trees making a pale green haze against the darker conifers. I said, "I'm Irene Fonsell, Mr. Fonsell's daughter-in-law."

He looked at me again and nodded, his dark eyes neither friendly nor unfriendly. I said, "Well, I'll leave you to your painting."

"Stay if you want. Unfold that thing and sit down. Talk doesn't bother me."

When I was seated I said, "I thought you painted only portraits."

"I used to. I don't do many portraits these days."

After a moment I ventured, "Why?"

"Too many sitters thought they looked different from the way I saw them. But a landscape never complains."

"I don't see how Mrs. Fonsell could have complained."

"She didn't." He placed his brush in the easel slot, and picked up a larger one.

"I think it's a fine portrait."

"It's all right."

"You know she was—murdered, don't you?"

"Of course. It was in the New York papers."

I hesitated, and then asked, "What was she like, besides being beautiful?"

He shrugged. "All I knew about her is there on the canvas."

Again I hesitated. "Then she must have struck you as sad. In the portrait there's an almost haunted look in her eyes."

Not speaking, he nodded.

"Did she ever talk about herself?"

"No, thank God. Most sitters do. I guess they want the painter to know how noble and generous and long-suffering they are, so that he can put all that on canvas. That's another

83

reason I stopped doing portraits. The money wasn't worth it."

He placed a highlight on one of the jagged planks in the foreground, and then added, "Not that the Fonsells paid me anything, as you probably know."

I hadn't known, but I had wondered about that. Ever since the disastrous turn in his fortunes back in 1847, Ephraim Fonsell had lived on income from a few government bonds, and the sale of parcels of Long Island real estate he had acquired in his prosperous days. It had seemed strange that he had been able to afford one of America's highest-priced painters.

"You mean you offered to paint her portrait because she was so beautiful?"

"Not just that. Her face interested me. I met her and her husband while I was spending a few days over at Noyack in a cottage a cousin of mine owned." Noyack was a small settlement about three miles from Sag Harbor. "I told the Fonsells that if she'd come to New York every week for a couple of months, I'd paint her portrait."

"Then you didn't paint it here?"

"Lord, no. Even sitters who paid me had to come to my studio. It was a rule of mine."

In those days, the spring and summer after the War ended, there had been no railroad connecting eastern Long Island with New York. She must have gone there and back by packet boat, which meant that she had been away from home at least three days of every week while John Solum was painting her portrait.

"Do you know where she stayed in New York?"

"Somewhere south of Washington Square," he said vaguely, "with a distant relative of hers, a Mrs. Smithers, or something like that. Anyway, the woman gave singing lessons."

For a while, neither of us spoke. Shifting my gaze from his canvas, I watched a three-masted bark, its white sails bellying in the wind as it made for Long Wharf. Finally I asked, "Are you staying in Noyack now?"

"I live there. My cousin died a few months ago and left his cottage to me."

"You don't go to New York at all any more?"

"Not often." He laid down his brush and turned to look at me. "I still do children's portraits sometimes. I'd say that your child will probably be worth painting."

I stiffened with shock. Even with female friends, one discussed one's condition only in discreet tones. For him, a man, and a strange man at that, to make such a direct reference to it was outrageous. If he noticed my reaction, he gave no sign. Turning back to his canvas, he picked up a brush.

My indignation cooled. After all, most people would say it had been improper of me to walk along the beach at this time, let alone sit here talking to a strange man. And anyway, he was a New Yorker and an artist. Such people didn't have the usual standards.

Besides, it would be gratifying indeed to have my little son, my little daughter, painted by John R. Solum.

"I don't know how much I could pay you." The few railroad stocks my mother had left me gave me an income of less than a hundred a year. And it was hard to imagine Jason diverting any of my aunt's money to a portrait painter.

John Solum shrugged. "If I decide to do the portrait, we'll work something out."

"In the meantime, wouldn't you like to come up to the house and look at your portrait of Mrs. Fonsell?"

He said indifferently, "I might, sometime."

"Perhaps you could come next Tuesday night, around six-thirty. We're celebrating my father-in-law's birthday."

The celebration had been my aunt's idea. I think that she was trying, for her own sake as well as mine, to create the illusion that ours was a normal household. And a normal household, of course, would not allow the seventy-second birthday of its patriarch to go unmarked by some sort of celebration.

"Maybe I'll be there. I can't promise."

Rising, I gathered up the folding stool. "Do come if you can."

Before I started up the path that led through the trees to the house, I looked back. Apparently as absorbed in his work as if our conversation had never taken place, he stood brush in hand, gaze fixed on his canvas.

Chapter 11

ENTERING THE WALLED garden through its wooden gate, I found Ephraim sitting near the flower bed from which, these last few days, I had pulled the dried skeletons of last year's blooms. He had a lap robe over his knees. Now that the weather had warmed, he often sat out here. As I have said, he was not a sensitive man. But the sight of him, calmly sunning himself within a few feet of where someone had beaten his wife to death, never failed to shock me.

I said, "Guess who was down at the cove. John R. Solum."

"Solum, Solum. Oh, sure. He painted Julia's portrait. Sit down and tell me about him."

I placed the folding stool on the flagstones. "He's living over in Noyack now, in a cottage a cousin of his left him."

"Maybe he'd like to come for my birthday." Ever since my aunt had proposed a birthday dinner, he had seemed to look forward to it with an almost childlike enthusiasm.

"I asked him. He may come."

"Jason may be here too. He wrote from Philadelphia. Mrs. Burlow brought the letter from the post office about an hour ago."

Vaguely I recalled hearing that Jason, unable to come to terms with the owner of the brig in the Brooklyn shipyard, had gone to Philadelphia to look at some schooners which were up for sale.

"What else did this painter fellow have to say?"

I hesitated. It would seem untactful to tell him I knew

now that he had paid nothing for his wife's portrait. "He didn't say much."

The bright old eyes looked at me shrewdly. "Come on. He said something about Julia, didn't he?"

"Only that she impressed him as rather sad."

He looked straight ahead for a moment and then nodded. "She had her reasons." He turned back to me. "I guess you've wondered why a woman like Julia married a rounder more than twice her age."

I said, embarrassed, "I never asked you that."

"I don't mind telling you. In 1852 I went up to Kennebunk, Maine. I hoped I could buy into a fleet of fishing boats there. Nothing came of it. I didn't have enough money to interest them. But I did meet Julia. She was twenty-two, and living with a spinster cousin of her mother's. Withering on the vine, so to speak, with no prospects of a husband."

Silently I wondered why.

"Not her fault," he went on. "Not any of it. Thing was, her grandfather had been in the slave trade, back before 1808, when it was legal. Her father and her brother stayed in it, after it was outlawed. Oh, most of the time their brig carried legitimate cargo. But every once in a while it would visit the African coast and then sail for the West Indies. The last time, a British gunboat closed in on it off Barbados. The brig tried to jettison cargo, but they weren't able to finish the job before the British came aboard."

Jettison cargo, I thought, feeling sick. I pictured the chained, helpless men and women and children thrust screaming over the ship's rail into shark-infested water.

"The gunboat took the brig's officers and crew back to England and tried them. Julia's father died in prison there. The brother was released after ten years, but he never went back to Maine. Nobody's sure where he went. Australia, maybe."

No wonder he had never returned to Maine. My aunt

had told me that the people of the New England states, most of them Abolitionists, had felt a particular loathing for their fellow New Englanders who made huge profits in the slave trade.

"Julia was only a young girl when her father and brother were caught. No one in Kennebunk blamed her. But none of the young men in town wanted in-laws like her father and brother, either. When I came along, I guess she figured I was her first and last chance. Anyway, she married me."

I hoped she had found some measure of content here in this Long Island house, with her two blond, handsome children. I even found myself hoping that Mrs. Burlow was right, that during the last weeks of Julia Fonsell's life, the aura of some secret joy had hovered around her. Perhaps when she stepped from this house into the moonlight the last night of her life, that happiness had glowed in her violet eyes . . .

Suddenly I felt I could not stay in this garden a moment longer. Getting to my feet, I picked up the folding stool. "Well, I have work waiting for me indoors."

By the next afternoon the weather had turned much colder. It remained so for several days. On the morning of Ephraim's birthday snow flurries filled the air outside the kitchen where Mrs. Burlow and my aunt and Ruth and I were preparing vegetables to accompany the roast, and baking the big birthday cake. My aunt commented worriedly that if too much snow fell, Dr. Ronsard might not want to drive over from Southampton. Ephraim, poking his head around the edge of the kitchen door, expressed the same fear.

I could understand their anxiety. Unless John R. Solum chose to honor us, Paul Ronsard would be our only guest. No one else had been invited. Ever since his wife's death, Ephraim had been shunned by the townspeople, and had shunned them in turn. And my aunt, obviously, had not wanted to embarrass any of her old friends, not even Dr.

Cantrell, by extending an invitation they might not want to accept. Looking at her thin, intent face above the birthday cake, and remembering how she used to enjoy giving teas for the friends she had known since girlhood, I felt a stab of guilty sorrow. True, she still sat in the Haverly pew each Sunday. True, she could go over to her beloved Howard Street house to air it out every month. But otherwise, she was almost as much of an exile as if she and I had gone to California.

We need not have worried, though, about the weather. Shortly after twelve the sun came out, and less than two hours later no trace of the light snowfall remained.

Jason came home on the late afternoon train. Apparently he still remembered, and resented, his clash with Paul Ronsard at the dinner table, because as I moved along the lower hall to arouse my aunt from her nap, I heard Jason's angry voice from behind the closed door of his father's den. "You always call him that damned sawbones. And yet you're having him here for your birthday!"

Ephraim's answer was an indistinct rumble. I walked on, wondering why Jason so resented Paul. Was it merely that the two men were of such different temperaments? Or was there some other reason? Well, no matter. Jason would surely have the decency not to make a scene at his father's birthday dinner. And tomorrow, or at least in a few days, probably he would be gone again.

At my aunt's door I tapped lightly and then, at her response, entered the room. She had not lit the gas lamps. Early evening shadows were so thick that a second or so passed before I saw her, a small, fragile figure seated in one of the slipper chairs.

"Did you have a good nap?" I asked. Then, as I moved toward her, I saw the big Bible open in her lap. "Aunt Elizabeth! You're not trying to read in this—"

I broke off. Her white, upturned face was trying to smile,

but her eyes were two dark pools of shock. I said, "What is it? What's happened?"

"Why, nothing, dear. But you and the others will have to excuse me tonight. I have a terrible headache."

"It's more than that!" I could not only see something akin to horror in her face, I could feel it around me in the shadowy room. "Something has happened."

Her slight figure drew itself up. "Irene, you are not to contradict me."

"Very well. But if you feel too ill to attend the party tonight, we'll have it tomorrow." I started to turn away. "I'll tell the others."

"Irene!" It was a low, frightened cry. I turned back. "You're to say nothing to anyone except that I don't feel well. You're to have the party just as if nothing had—just as if I were at the table."

So something had happened. Whatever it was—whatever she had seen, or heard, or otherwise learned—it had happened within the last hour and a half. It was not until four-thirty that she had left the kitchen, obviously looking forward to the evening's festivities, and gone to her room to take a nap.

I said, "If you'd just tell me—"

She abandoned pretense. "All right. I am—disturbed about something. Perhaps I'll come to your room tonight to talk to you about it. Or perhaps I'll wait until tomorrow. But there's no need to upset you now. In fact, it's important that you not be upset."

Not be upset. Not convey to others that acute distress she had conveyed to me.

"Please, Irene. Trust me. Please do just as I say."

I looked around the darkening room. Julia Fonsell's room. Had my aunt learned something about Julia, something that others must not suspect she knew? "All right," I said reluctantly. "I'll do as you say."

I left her then, and went up to my room, and put on the dress my aunt and I had altered for the occasion. It was the same yellow taffeta I had worn to the ball in the Huntting Building more than a year ago, its waist considerably let out now, and with a concealing overskirt added. Fleetingly I wondered if Jason would recognize the dress, and recall those uncomfortable, mostly silent minutes when he had whirled me over the floor to the strains of *Artist's Life*.

I was brushing my hair when I heard Paul Ronsard's surrey drive below my window toward the carriage house. A few minutes later I descended the stairs.

I found the others assembled in the parlor, where Mrs. Burlow and I had opened windows earlier that day, removed slipcovers from horsehair sofas and chairs, and dusted the many small marble-topped tables. As I entered, Jason was standing beside the fireplace. I could tell by the sardonic expression in his eyes that he did remember the yellow dress.

Smiling regretfully, I made the little speech I had rehearsed. "My aunt asks to be excused. Perhaps she worked too hard today. Anyway, she has a bad headache. But she wants us to enjoy ourselves. She'll be very distressed if we don't."

I looked swiftly around the room, and saw sympathy and disappointment in every face, including Jason's. Paul Ronsard said, "Perhaps I should look in on her. I have my medical kit with me."

"No," I said quickly. "She's going to take a headache powder, and then try to sleep."

He nodded. "Best thing in the world for her."

Again my gaze swept the faces around me. Why, these people not only respected my aunt. They had grown fond of her. Surely she could not be afraid of any of these four.

Then I realized that her fear need not have been of any of the Fonsells or of Paul Ronsard. Mrs. Burlow was part of this household too. And there were at least two others—

Annabelle Clyssom and Jason's mother—who had once lived in this house. Perhaps my aunt had been anxious that I not communicate her fear to Jason, lest he tell Annabelle about it. I thought, too, of our hoped-for guest, the distinguished portrait painter whom my aunt, at least until late this afternoon, had been so eager to meet. True, he had never lived in this house, but he had known Julia Fonsell shortly before her tragic death.

I became aware of Ephraim's shrewd old eyes fixed upon me. With a bright smile I asked, "No word from Mr. Solum yet? Well, perhaps he'll be here soon."

We were sipping the "lady's drink," Madeira, which Jason had poured into thin glasses when Mrs. Burlow appeared in the doorway. I saw her gaze dart around in search of my aunt. "Dinner is served."

"Will you hold dinner back for fifteen minutes, Mrs. Burlow? We might be having another guest."

She nodded. But her tightened lips conveyed her opinion that in fifteen minutes the roast would be tough and the vegetables soggy.

"And please remove Miss Haverly's plate," I said. "She's not feeling well."

After fifteen minutes John Solum had not arrived, and so we went in to dinner. The slight delay had ruined neither the roast nor the vegetables. Still, the dinner was not a success. Perhaps, in spite of my best efforts not to, I communicated my puzzled unease to the others. Whatever the reason, I was aware of a growing tension around the table. There were periods of silence that even Paul Ronsard seemed at a loss to fill.

At last Mrs. Burlow brought in the three-layer cake. "Good. No candles," Ephraim joked. "That many candles might have set the house afire."

There should have been at least one candle. I recalled my aunt saying, just before she left the kitchen that afternoon,

"Well, it's all done except for the pink candle for the cake. I'll bring it back here after my nap. Ruth, when you helped me unpack, where did you put that box of candles?"

"On the shelf of your wardrobe," Ruth said, and I had smiled, realizing that my thrifty aunt must have brought from the Howard Street house the box of candles, many of them partially consumed, which had graced my own childhood birthday parties.

But she had not returned to the kitchen with the candle.

Because this was supposed to be an occasion, we drank our coffee in the parlor. At nine Paul Ronsard, with the ten-mile journey to Southampton ahead of him, said good night, and went back along the hall to the rear door and the carriage house beyond. A few minutes after we heard him drive away, I too excused myself.

At the foot of the stairs I hesitated, looking toward my aunt's door. Should I see if she were awake? No, I decided, remembering the urgency with which she had said, "Irene, please do just as I say." She would come to my room in her own time, she had told me, either tonight or tomorrow morning.

In my room I tried to read Jane Austen's *Emma,* my ears alert for Aunt Elizabeth's light step on the stairs. The sound did not come. I heard Ephraim's slow, heavy tread as he passed my door toward his room, and then Ruth's lighter one on the opposite side of the hall. After that, silence. No sound from Jason, apparently still somewhere on the ground floor, or from the room directly below mine, where, I hoped, my aunt now slept. At last I laid my book aside and undressed.

I must have been more tired than I had realized, because soon after I lay down my uneasy thoughts became diffused, and blurred into sleep.

In my dream I moved along the cove's sandy edge, through a pearly fog that made the foot or so of visible water, lapping at the sand, look black. "Please, Miss Haverly," a soft voice behind me said, "please let me talk to you." Miss Haverly. So the speaker must be someone who had been away, someone who did not know my legal name was no longer Haverly. I turned, wondering if the owner of the soft voice had been a man or a woman, and waiting for a dark figure to take shape in the fog.

A sound. Out in the hall. I sat up in bed, the pearly mist of my dream dissolving, and that sound—a sort of strangled cry—echoing in my ears. And hadn't it been followed by another sound, a muffled one, as if something had fallen?

Heart pounding, hands icy with fear, I got out of bed and struggled into my dressing gown. Usually a light was left burning in the first floor hall, but someone must have turned it out, because no thread of light showed beneath my door. Matches, where were matches? My searching hand found them on the bedside table. I ran out into the pitch-black hall, groped for the wall sconce, turned it on, and lit it. Then I started down the stairs.

A few steps below the landing I halted, looking down over the banister. On the floor down there, looking small as a child, my aunt lay huddled in her brown bombazine dress.

Chapter 12

SHE WAS STILL ALIVE when I reached her. As I knelt there, cold with terror, her dazed eyes looked up at me. "Thrown," she said. "Didn't fall. Thrown."

"Who was it?" I pressed her thin hand between both of mine. "Who was it?"

Her struggle to marshal thoughts, words, was plain in her dimming eyes. She drew a ragged breath. "London," she said urgently. She managed to reach out with her other hand and shake my arm. "From *London*," she repeated, but there was despair in her face, as if she knew that she had not found the right words to convey her meaning. Then her hand fell from my sleeve, and all the light went out of her eyes, and I knew that she was dead.

This house, I thought. This murderous house. In my hysteria it seemed to me that I could feel cold evil all around me, swirling up the stairwell to push against the gray-green bubble. I heard a voice screaming for help, and after a second or two knew that it was mine. But I did not get to my feet. I went on kneeling there, dimly aware that tears poured down my face.

People around me now. Ephraim and Ruth, in dressing gowns. Jason, fully dressed. Mrs. Burlow in a brown bathrobe, hurrying from the foot of the back stairs along the lower hall. "Someone killed her," I said. "Someone killed her."

"Irene, get up from there." Jason's voice. Jason's hands, grasping my upper arms to lift me to my feet. I looked up into his dark face. And through my grief and terror came one clear, cold thought. "He has it all now." From now on Fonsell and Haverly, Incorporated, would be just Fonsell.

Perhaps the thought showed in my face, because a flush made his own face even darker. Bending, he put one arm beneath my knees and swept me from my feet. As he carried me up the stairs, I heard him shout over his shoulder, "Ruth! Bring some laudanum to her room. And Mrs. Burlow, drive across the bridge and bring Dr. Cantrell back with you."

Sometime in the night I awoke to light dimmed by a tall screen placed in front of the gas fixture. Dr. Cantrell, eyes worried behind rimless glasses, sat in the chair beside my bed.

"Someone killed her," I said. "Someone killed my—"

"No one killed her." Hands on my shoulders, he forced me to lower my head to the pillow. "Your aunt had a stroke."

"She didn't! Someone—"

"Irene, I can tell when someone has suffered a stroke! She fell, too, and that's what actually killed her. She broke her neck. But it was the stroke that caused her fall. She must have staggered against the banister, become overbalanced—"

"But she said—"

"A stroke victim, if he can speak at all, may say anything. It's like an explosion in the brain. Now listen, Irene." His smooth-shaven, jowly face was stern. "Your aunt's dead. Do you want your child to be dead too?"

I moved my lips in a silent no.

"Then try to be as calm as you can. I'm going to give you another sleeping potion, a light one."

As I watched him place his black leather satchel on a chair, I thought of what he had said. Perhaps my aunt had suffered a second stroke. But I was sure that someone had caused that stroke. Someone who had called softly, as she climbed toward my room, "Miss Haverly! Please let me talk to you." He had hurried up the stairs, and put his hand over her mouth to stifle her cry. Then, lifting her frail body high above the banister . . .

"Irene! Take this." Obediently I swallowed the liquid he had measured into a glass.

When I again awoke, it was to the ironical brightness of a beautiful spring day. Dr. Cantrell had gone. Instead it was Rose Murphy who stood at the window, lowering a shade against the sunlight.

I said, thankfulness mingling with my grief, "Oh, Rose. You're here."

She hurried toward me. Her eyes, I saw, were red-rimmed. "I came as soon as I heard. And I'm going to stay, no matter what." I realized that already she must have clashed with someone in this house, probably Mrs. Burlow. "Now you're not to fret, love. You're to stay in bed for at least three days. Dr. Cantrell said so."

"When is—when will Aunt Elizabeth—"

"The funeral is Friday. But you're not to go. You can understand that, can't you, love?"

I said dully, "Yes." After a moment I went on, "Rose, she told me she didn't fall. Someone threw her over that banister."

"Now, dearie—"

"Rose, listen! I asked who it was. I guess the stroke had confused her so that she couldn't give me the name. But she did try to tell me something. She said, 'London, from London.'"

"Folks who've had a stroke are apt to say almost anything." Obviously, Dr. Cantrell had told her how to handle me. "And what could London have to do with it?"

I did not know. But Mrs. Burlow's accent indicated that she had been born within the sound of Bow bells. And there was something else—oh, yes. Poor Julia Fonsell's father and brother had been tried and sentenced by an English court.

And there was still something else, something that Aunt

Prudence had said on one of those languorous afternoons when she sat in the dim light that filtered through the jalousies, waving a palm leaf fan as she reminisced about Sag Harbor. She had mentioned London in some connection. What was it, what was it?

"There you go, fretting again," Rose said. "I can tell by your face. I'm going down now and fix your breakfast with my own hands, no matter what that Mrs. Burlow says. What would you like?"

Late Friday afternoon Rose told me that the church literally had been filled to overflowing for my aunt's funeral. Some people, unable to find seats, had stood in the vestibule throughout the service. Perhaps sheer curiosity over a second violent death in the Fonsell house had drawn a few of them. But most, I felt sure, had been there to pay their last respects to a fine woman, and I took comfort from their having done so.

That night was the first since my aunt's death that Dr. Cantrell had ordered no sleeping draught for me. I lay wide awake in the dark, hearing the big clock in the downstairs hall strike eleven, then midnight, then one, and trying not to wonder what my aunt had been coming up the stairs to tell me, trying not to speculate as to who might have prevented her from reaching me. A stroke, Dr. Cantrell had said. A stroke, and then a fall. For my sake and my child's, that was what it was best for me to believe. That was what I wanted to believe.

Then, my body suddenly taut, I knew I could not believe that. Because in the room directly below mine some object had fallen with a soft thud. I raised my head to listen. For perhaps two minutes there was silence, broken only by the seething sound of my own blood. Then I heard a faint squeak. That top drawer of the mahogany bureau in the room below. Even though my aunt had rubbed the drawer's edges with wax, it still squeaked when pulled open.

Someone was down there, searching the room that had been my aunt's and, before her, Julia Fonsell's. I threw back the covers, and very carefully swung my feet to the floor. I moved across the carpet toward the window, praying that no complaint of a floor board would betray me, and looked down through the window screen.

Across the graveled drive that led back to the carriage house lay a narrow strip of light. Plainly the draperies at the French doors, drawn together by the searcher, did not quite meet. And he had left at least one of the doors open, because the faint night wind, stirring the draperies, made the edges of that ribbon of light waver. I stood there, only dimly aware of the chill striking through my nightgown, and strained to listen.

Another thud, a softer one. The lid of that Chinese chest, opening back against the wall? A brushing sound, as if someone were sweeping ashes from the fireplace onto its brick apron, searching for half-burned scraps of paper. The first two tinkling notes, abruptly silenced, of "O Christmas Tree." I could imagine the faceless searcher, frightened now, standing with his hand on the music box lid, his ears listening as hard as mine listened.

Then the strip of light vanished from the drive.

Heart pounding, I moved swiftly across the room and got into bed. With my back turned to the door, I closed my eyes tight. If in another moment someone moved softly up the stairs and opened the door of this room, I must, for my own safety, appear sound asleep.

I listened, but heard nothing except the thud of my own heart. No stealthy opening of the door below, no footsteps on the stairs. But he was no longer in that room. I sensed its emptiness. He must have silently opened the door of my aunt's room and, in stockinged feet, made his way back along the lower hall, perhaps to another downstairs room, or perhaps up the back stairs to this floor, or the one above.

Or was it a woman who had slipped out of that room? I thought of Mrs. Burlow—"I've always been light on my feet" —in her old brown bathrobe, and of tall, slender Ruth gliding along the lower hall.

Downstairs the clock struck two. My heartbeats had slowed now, and yet I knew, staring into the blackness, that I would not sleep until daylight.

Chapter 13

LATE MORNING SUNLIGHT was flooding my room when I finally awoke. Knitting an infant's cap of cream-colored wool, Rose sat in a chair near the window. "Rose."

"So you finally woke up, sleepyhead." She placed her knitting on the small table beside her and moved toward me. "A bad night?"

"Bad dreams." Before I fell asleep, I had decided not to tell her, or anyone, about those sounds in the night—at least not until I'd had the chance to look over my aunt's room.

"Rose, it's a lot to ask, but could you sleep in this room for at least a few nights? I'd feel better if you were here."

"Of course I will, love. There must be a light cot somewhere in this house. I'll set it up in here."

I hesitated. "Rose, about your salary. I'm afraid I—"

"It's all arranged. The Biemeyers say I can stay here as long as I'm needed. And Mr. Fonsell will take care of my pay. Young Mr. Fonsell, that is. He told me so."

"He's still here?"

She nodded. "I heard him telling old Mr. Fonsell that he'd changed his mind about going back to Philadelphia right away. Now I'll fix your breakfast. And later today, if you don't mind being left alone for a while, I'll cross the bridge and collect the rest of my things from the Biemeyers." She paused. "How does some toast and soft-boiled eggs sound?"

"Wonderful. While you're in the kitchen I think I'll get dressed."

She nodded. "Dr. Cantrell told me yesterday at—at the church that you could get up today, if you felt like it. He also said he'd be here to see you around two-thirty this afternoon."

Around one o'clock, a few minutes after I heard the heavy front door close behind Rose, I quietly left my room and went down the stairs. If I encountered anyone, I intended to say that I wanted a book from my aunt's room. But the lower hall was empty. I entered my aunt's room and closed the door behind me.

The heavy draperies were still drawn at the French windows. As I crossed through the dim light, a length of drapery bellied inward. One of the windows must still be open. For the first time I realized that it need not have been a member of this household who had searched this room the night before. Anyone could have entered through that window and then left the same way, moving silently over the strip of grass that bordered the graveled drive.

Trying to rattle the metal rings as little as possible, I pushed the draperies apart. Reaching out, I grasped the iron handle, and softly closed the French window's open half. There was a bolt about a foot above the two handles. I pushed it into place.

Turning, I surveyed the room, now flooded with light. Nothing seemed out of place. No, one thing was. The little footstool that matched the two slipper chairs flanking the fireplace now stood beside that deep, eight-foot-high wardrobe. Of course, I thought. The box of candles. My aunt, unlike Ruth, would have needed to stand on something to reach the wardrobe shelf.

Still moving quietly, I opened the wardrobe's heavily carved doors. My aunt's cloaks and dresses, suspended from padded hangers, had been pushed toward one end. At the opposite end, high up, was a little corner shelf.

I saw now that I too would need the footstool. Placing

it on the wardrobe's sturdy planked floor, I mounted it, and felt around on the shelf until my groping fingers found the tin box. Still standing on the footstool, I took the box down and opened it. Yes, here were the pink candles so evocative of my growing-up years. I closed the lid, replaced the box, and then, as my aunt must have done, stepped forward and to my right off the stool.

With a scraping noise, the opposite end of the plank upon which my right toe pressed moved several inches up the wardrobe's rear wall. Startled, I withdrew my foot. The plank settled back into place. Then, again as my aunt must have done, I set the footstool outside the wardrobe. Pulse rapid now, I knelt on the wardrobe floor and placed the heel of my hand on the right end of the loose plank. The other end scraped upward. The nails that had fastened this board to the studding below must have been taken out, because without difficulty I lifted the six-inch-wide length of wood and, reaching outside the wardrobe, placed it on the carpet.

I looked down at the strip of the room's flooring I had revealed. Apparently this massive wardrobe had not been moved for years, because the dust lay thick and gray down there except in one spot. Near the center of the revealed strip was a dust-free rectangle about four inches by six inches.

Something had lain there, hidden, under the loose plank. A small box, perhaps. Whatever it was, had my aunt placed it there? Or had she been unaware of its existence until, like me, she had stepped down from the stool onto that loose board? In either case, where was it now? Had my aunt hidden it somewhere else in this room? And the searcher, I thought, my nerves tightening with the memory of last night's fear. Had he been looking for whatever had lain beneath that loose plank?

Reaching out, I picked up the plank and fitted it back into the wardrobe floor. I got to my feet, moved out onto the Aubusson, and stood for a moment looking at Aunt Elizabeth's brown and black and dark green garments. Apparently they had been disturbed by my movements, because they swayed gently on their hangers. Swaying with the others was the brown bombazine she had worn as she climbed toward my room on Tuesday night to tell me—what?

Behind me, the door opened. Pulse leaping in my throat, I turned around. Mrs. Burlow stood there, a broom in one hand and a dustpan in the other. Her pinched face looked disconcerted. "Why, Mrs. Fonsell! What are you doing down here?"

I said, as calmly as I could, "I intend to sort out my aunt's clothing. Most of it will go over to the church for distribution to the poor. Will you pack them for me?"

"Right now? I wanted to sweep this room."

"No, not right now. And would you mind not sweeping just yet? I'm not through in here."

As always when I interfered with her routine, Mrs. Burlow looked injured. I went on, "I found one of the French windows open. Do you know how that happened?"

"Dr. Cantrell opened that door! Tuesday night, after they carried your aunt in here!" Her voice took on that defensive whine. "I know I should have closed it. But I can't do everything. And the last few days have been bad. You not able to help. And now that Rose Murphy coming into my kitchen at all hours."

"I realize you can't do everything. But except when you air the room out, I'd like these doors to be latched."

She nodded sullenly.

"And the back and front doors of this house are to be locked at night from now on. There are keys, I suppose."

"Somewhere. I'll have to look for them. We never locked doors before."

"Well, I'd like them to be locked at night now."

"What are you going to do with her other things?" Her gaze moved around the room, lingering with what seemed to me a touch of cupidity on my aunt's silver-backed brush and hand mirror.

"Nothing. They'll remain here for the time being."

My child, if a girl, would own that brush and mirror someday.

"Well," she said, backing into the hall, "I guess I'll go see to Mr. Ephraim's room."

She closed the door. I moved swiftly about, not bothering now to avoid noise. Soon the whole household would know that Mrs. Fonsell had been "poking around in her aunt's room," so further caution was useless. I opened bureau drawers. Obviously last night's searcher had been careful indeed, because underwear and nightgowns lay in neat stacks. If the object responsible for that dust-free rectangle under the loose plank had been placed in this bureau, it was no longer here. I opened the Chinese chest, releasing an odor of camphor, and searched vainly through the folded cashmere and hand-knitted shawls. While the music box played "O Christmas Tree," I looked at its contents—the cameo my aunt sometimes wore, and the jet earrings, opal ring, and strings of coral beads she never wore. All of that jewelry had been inherited from Grandmother Haverly, who evidently had been of more frivolous tastes than her elder daughter.

The hall clock struck two, its bronze voice vibrating in the silence. Soon Dr. Cantrell would be here. I went out into the hall and climbed the stairs.

In my room about forty minutes later, I told Dr. Cantrell of the sounds I had heard the night before, and my search of my aunt's room today. As I talked, I saw growing disapproval in his face.

At last he said, "Irene, why must you put the most disturbing interpretation on everything?"

"Don't you believe I heard someone down there?"

"Yes." Taking off his glasses, he polished their lenses with a white handkerchief. "But don't you realize that from a legal point of view, everyone in this house had a right to go into that room?"

I said, disconcerted, "But to search through my aunt's things—"

"That was reprehensible, of course, but not surprising. Mrs. Burlow is a woman of avid curiosity. And Ruth—well, who knows what goes on in that poor girl's head?"

"You think it was Ruth, or Mrs. Burlow?"

"Doesn't that seem likely? At that hour Ephraim was probably sleeping the sleep of the just and the drunken. And I find it hard to imagine Jason being that curious. He's too busy trying to get rich."

But, I wanted to say, he might have thought that room held something dangerous to him. I didn't say it, though, lest I lead the conversation down a bypath. Instead I said, "I found one of the French windows open down there."

"Still? I opened it Tuesday night. It was stuffy, with everyone crowding into the room."

"A person could have stepped in there last night, without the risk of coming through other parts of the house."

"What person? I, for instance, after leaving the door conveniently open for my return?"

I found myself smiling. "Not you. You weigh so much that I would have heard every footstep."

"Thank you for the exoneration." He put his glasses back on. "Whom do you suspect then? My colleague, Paul Ronsard? Do you imagine it was an eminent man of medicine snooping through your aunt's belongings?"

I said defensively, "It could have been. He could have had some reason. But I was thinking of Annabelle Clyssom."

He shot me a searching look, as if to gauge whether or not I resented Jason's continuing relationship with Annabelle. Then he shook his head. "She's a bold baggage, that one. Sneaking just isn't her style. It's the women with no real life of their own who snoop around in other people's lives."

Perhaps he was right. But again, if she had some urgent reason— I said, "I also thought of Jason's mother."

"Jason's mother! Why, she lives thirty miles away. And as far as I know, she hasn't been near this house for more than twenty years."

"As far as you know! That's just it, Dr. Cantrell. Someone killed Julia Fonsell almost ten years ago, and if it wasn't that poor lunatic, then probably it was someone connected with this house."

I leaned forward. "Don't you see? Suppose my aunt found something under that floorboard, something that explained Julia Fonsell's death. Suppose someone guessed that she—"

"Guessed? How?"

"I don't know how. I only know that before that birthday dinner Tuesday night, she seemed upset, frightened."

"Of course she was. After her first light stroke she described to me, with her usual precision, just how she had felt before it happened. The dizziness, the sense of pressure in her head, and so on. Tuesday night she must have realized another stroke might be impending. Naturally she was frightened, not just for herself, but for you also. What was more, she realized that what she most needed was quiet. She didn't want you to alarm the others, ruin Ephraim's birthday party, and throw the whole house into a turmoil."

While I was turning his words over in my mind, he went on, "Do you know what I think was under that floorboard? A packet of letters your aunt had saved. Probably when she moved into this house she found that loose board, and decided to conceal the letters under it."

I realized now that the dust-free rectangle had been about the size of an envelope. "But my aunt never saved letters. She said they made clutter. She destroyed letters as soon as she answered them."

"Ordinary letters, perhaps. But suppose they were love

letters? Or does it seem impossible to one of your tender years that your aunt could ever have received love letters?"

"Of course it doesn't seem impossible! And I know that there was someone she once wanted to marry. She told me so." After a moment I went on, "And if there were love letters there, you think Mrs. Burlow or Ruth may have found them?" I shrank from the thought of either of those two reading with coldly curious eyes letters from the only man my aunt had ever loved, a man she hadn't discussed even with me.

"Perhaps. Or perhaps your aunt, with a strong premonition of her death, took them from their hiding place and burned them."

I hesitated, and then asked, "Were you the man my aunt loved?"

"No, nor did I write her any letters. But some years ago, after my wife died, I asked your aunt to marry me."

I said, startled, "What did she say?"

"She told me that long ago she had resolved never to make a middle-aged fool of herself. And in the most tactful manner possible, she advised me to make the same resolution."

I was begining to feel I had made a young fool of myself. It appeared probable now that my aunt's assailant had had no existence outside her hemorrhage-stricken brain. It also appeared that there had been no reason for me to flee back to my bed the night before, to lie there with eyes squeezed shut, and heart thudding with fear that soon I would hear my door stealthily open. The searcher of the room below had been either an embittered middle-aged woman or a sly and secretive young one, hoping to find, now that my aunt was dead, that her upright life had held some titillating secret.

Dr. Cantrell said, "Irene, I've been thinking. I'd hate you to have the upset of moving right now. But even so, perhaps you'd be better off if you and Rose Murphy went back to the Howard Street house, at least until your child is born. If you like, I'll speak to Jason about it."

When I didn't answer, he went on, "Considering the shock you've experienced here, I don't see how he could possibly object, and if he does, I'll deal with him. I can always threaten to tell people that he insisted on your staying here, despite your wishes and despite your doctor's advice. I don't imagine he'll want more scandal about the Fonsells spread around."

I shook my head. Like Jason, I wanted no more scandal, not if my child was to grow up in this town. And my moving from this house, in my present condition and only a few days after my aunt's death, would be sure to cause talk.

"I'll be all right. And I won't be afraid. Rose is going to sleep in this room, at least for a few nights."

"Good girl." Rising, he patted my shoulder. "Now if you'll just try to keep a quiet mind, and follow your diet, and get a little mild exercise each day, you'll be fine."

Chapter 14

THE NEXT FEW WEEKS, during which I tried to follow Dr. Cantrell's advice, passed quietly. No sounds rose at night from the room below, and soon I stopped listening for them. At the end of the first week, I told Rose that I no longer felt uneasy, and so there was no need for her to sleep on that narrow cot. The truth was that although fear no longer kept me awake, her snores did.

In the daytime I read, knitted a crib blanket, and took walks down to the cove, usually accompanied by Rose. One afternoon I looked up the narrow beach and saw John Solum standing at his easel. Intent upon his painting—a landscape of Sag Harbor rising from the bay to its low hills, to judge by the direction in which he faced—he did not even turn his head in my direction.

For the first week after my aunt's death, reluctant to face the others at dinner, I had continued to take my meals from trays Rose brought to my room. But finally I resumed going downstairs in the evening. Jason was there for dinner that night, and for at least two nights out of three thereafter. Evidently, at least for the time being, his business affairs did not demand his presence elsewhere. He and I scarcely spoke or even looked at each other. I could not forget the bitter thought that had flashed through my mind as he lifted me from beside my aunt's body, and he, apparently, could not forget the reflection of that thought in my face.

The first Wednesday after I resumed coming downstairs in the evening, Paul Ronsard as usual stayed for dinner.

To my relief, he did not dwell upon my loss. He quietly expressed his sympathy, and then turned to the sort of pleasant talk which, I liked to think, had solaced my aunt for her exile from her Howard Street house.

Giving me surprisingly little trouble in the process, my dark-haired daughter—later christened Elizabeth, but from the first called Liza—was born one morning in late June.

When I awoke from the deep sleep into which I had fallen, I saw Rose across the room, bent raptly over the cradle which, two weeks before, had been brought down from the attic.

"Rose, I'm hungry."

She said, "Bless you," as if my hunger was some splendid achievement, and hurried over to the bed. "How do you feel, love?"

"I told you. Hungry as a wolf. How is Liza?"

"Asleep, the little angel. I'll go down and get your soup. I've had it simmering for three hours." She started toward the door, and then turned back. "Last time I was downstairs, Mr. Jason stopped me in the hall. He wants to know when he can see Liza. He's going away day after tomorrow."

A startling thought struck me. Could it be that what had held him close to home these past weeks was the impending birth of my child? "Tell him he can come tomorrow afternoon, if he likes."

Around two the next afternoon, face carefully expressionless, Rose admitted Jason to my room. He gave me an oddly formal little bow, asked how I was, and then walked over to where Rose, arms folded, stood beside the cradle. He said, after a moment, "She's asleep. I suppose she sleeps a lot."

Rose said coolly, "Young babies do."

He said, still looking down in the cradle, "What color are her eyes?"

"Blue," I said.

He turned his gaze to me. "Like Steven's." If I remembered correctly, it was the first time I had heard him refer to his brother since that morning in the parlor of the Howard Street house. After a moment he added, "I suppose you hoped she'd have blond hair."

"Yes. Now, of course, I wouldn't change anything about her."

There was a moment's silence. Then he said, "May I talk to you, alone?"

I said, "Rose . . ."

Grim-faced, she crossed the room. She said, hand on the knob, "I'll wait right outside."

When the door had closed behind her, Jason took a straight chair from the wall, placed it about three feet from my bed, and sat down. "It's about my partnership with your aunt. I suppose you know that I, as the surviving partner, am now sole owner of Fonsell and Haverly. That's the way the papers were drawn up."

"Yes," I said crisply, and waited.

"I intend to transfer your aunt's partnership to you."

After a moment I said, "Thank you. That's very generous of you." It was not generous. It was no more than fair. Still, it was something I had not expected.

"Just as before, the partnership will be indissoluble, except by mutual consent."

Or by death, I thought.

"But your share of the profits, as soon as there are any profits, will be entirely yours."

"Under any circumstances?"

"Under any circumstances."

In the weeks since my aunt's death I had often reflected that my freedom to get a divorce was an illusory one. How would I support myself and my child? Here at least I had food and shelter. But my aunt had left me only the Howard Street house and two parcels of land near the southern limits of the village, property which in these depressed times could not be sold for more than a few hundred dollars. All her other assets had gone into Fonsell and Haverly.

Even if Jason transferred my aunt's partnership to me, I would be no better off for some time to come. Little as I knew about business, I was sure that even if the firm succeeded, it would require many months or even years to show its first clear profits. But at least now I would have hope of eventual independence.

Why was he giving me that hope? Out of sheer generosity? That seemed unlikely, considering the hard bargain he had driven with my aunt and me. Or was it because he wanted me to be in a position to divorce him? That certainly could be. He might feel that he, once he had fulfilled his financial ambitions, would want to be free to contract a real marriage.

Or was he trying to appease some guilt, something that did not allow him to sleep of nights?

I said, "When will the agreement be drawn up?"

"It already has been, and I've signed it. It's in Clayton Yuill's law office now, waiting for your signature."

"Thank you," I said again.

He rose. "Well, I may not be here again for quite a while. I have a number of things to attend to."

"I hope everything goes well."

"I'm sure you do," he said, in a tone that added, "now." He put his hand on the doorknob. "Well, goodbye."

Like everyone else, I had always measured time by clock and calendar. But now I had a new means of measurement—

Liza. Liza's first real smile, the one Rose did not attribute to "gas on the stomach." The first time she reached for the rattle I dangled before her. The first time she sat up alone, the first time she distinctly said "Mama," her first wavering step.

I found myself surprisingly content. Content with Liza, and my household tasks, and my shopping forays across the bridge, and Paul Ronsard's entertaining presence on Wednesday nights, and the sometimes scandalous reminiscences in which my father-in-law indulged as I sat beside him, hands busy with knitting, out in the garden.

One chill March day when Liza was about nine months old, I encountered John Solum down at the cove. He stood clad in a moth-eaten greatcoat and a knitted red seaman's cap, painting the ice-scummed water and Long Wharf beyond. I said, "Why, hello. I haven't seen you for a long time."

He glanced at me and then turned his attention back to his canvas. "I've been in Europe."

"Where in Europe?"

"All over." I waited for him to make some explanation of his nonappearance at Ephraim's birthday party. Instead he asked, his gaze raking my now-slender figure, "Boy or girl?"

I thought, *"Really!"* Then I laughed and said, "A girl."

"How old?"

"She's nine months now."

"No good."

"What do you mean, no good?"

"At that age they have blobs for faces. But I might paint her seven or eight months from now, if she interests me."

I had to remind myself that this was John R. Solum, whose rudeness even Astors and Vanderbilts had endured. I said, "I still can't pay you much." The first Fonsell and Haverly vessel, an aged but sound brig which Jason had renamed the *Kestrel*, had yet to make its first voyage.

"That's all right. If I like what I see, I'll paint her. Maybe your husband and I can work something out about payment."

"My husband isn't here very often." Even when he was in the Harbor, he stayed away from the Fonsell house most of the time. I had no difficulty in guessing where he was.

John Solum said indifferently, "Oh? Well, we'll see." He turned back to his easel with an air which seemed to dismiss the subject.

"I'd better go," I said. "I have housework. Goodbye."

He looked at me, nodded, and then frowned at his canvas. Turning, I walked back to the house and my unfinished tasks.

I had grown no more intimate with either Mrs. Burlow or my sister-in-law. In Mrs. Burlow's case, I didn't want to. In Ruth's case, intimacy seemed impossible as well as undesirable. Often as I worked beside them, I wondered which one had taken my aunt's letters, if in fact such letters had existed. I found the whole matter so distasteful that I never made any reference to either woman, even an oblique one, about that nocturnal prowler in my aunt's room.

By late November the extensively reconditioned *Kestrel* was ready for her first voyage to the Caribbean. Jason took his father and sister and me aboard the brig as it lay alongside Long Wharf. His dark face holding an enthusiasm I had never seen there before, he pointed out the teakwood decks, the two masts, and the new sails furled along the yards. Below decks he showed us his own cabin and those of his officers, the four passenger cabins, and crew's quarters in the forecastle. I doubt that Ruth, following with her vague smile in her brother's wake, understood more than a little of his talk of flying jibs, stanchions, shifting boards, and braces. And I, even though a member of a seagoing family, could not grasp fully the workings of the auxiliary steam engine which would maneuver the *Kestrel* in and out of port.

Several days later Ephraim and Ruth and I returned to Long Wharf to watch the brig's departure on its three-month voyage. Sails tautened by a brisk west wind, it moved toward Cedar Point, looking as graceful as the bird for which it was named.

Some weeks passed before I realized that I had not seen Annabelle Clyssom on Main Street since before Jason sailed on the *Kestrel*. Had she, even as Ruth and Ephraim and I waved goodbye from the dock, been unpacking her luggage in one of the passenger cabins? No, not even Jason Fonsell would take her aboard in the Harbor, not when he was trying to build up local good will. But the brig had been scheduled to stop at a small Long Island port, Port Jefferson, for additional supplies. Probably she had met the ship there.

What Jason did ashore was his business. But the *Kestrel*, according to the papers I had signed in Lawyer Yuill's office, was half mine. For several days I went about my household tasks filled with a disturbing anger. Then I convinced myself that it really did not matter. What mattered was the money the *Kestrel* might earn eventually for Liza and me.

John Solum appeared at the front door one cold afternoon in late December, while I was waxing the downstairs hall. When he came in, wearing his shabby greatcoat and seaman's cap, he said, "I'm here to look at your little girl."

Delighted, I led him up to the nursery Rose and I had established in the room adjoining mine. Seated at her two-foot-high table in her little chair, Liza was finishing her lunch of vegetable stew. Rose stood beside the table, pouring milk from a pitcher into a mug.

I said, "Rose, this is the man I told you about, the one who may paint Liza's portrait. This is Miss Murphy, Mr. Solum."

Rose greeted him, bent to wipe a bit of carrot from Liza's chin, and then stood with folded arms, ready to beam or glare at him as his decision merited. He looked at Liza, and she looked calmly back at him from sooty-lashed blue eyes.

At last he said, "She'll do." He turned toward the door. "Now I'll decide where to paint her."

I said, hurrying to keep up as he descended the stairs, "Hadn't you better wait until June? She'll be older then, and there's this rambler rose climbing the western wall of the garden . . ." Liza in sheerest white lawn against the scarlet roses, dark curls bare but with a Leghorn hat lying on the grass beside her.

"I'll be busy next June." At the foot of the stairs he opened the parlor door. "What's in here?" Not waiting for my reply he said, "This will do."

I followed him into the parlor. "But we almost never use this room. And it's so cold in here."

"It certainly is. I'll be here at ten tomorrow. Have a fire burning in this room from seven o'clock on. Better make it six."

While I was absorbing that, he went on, "Don't dress her up. Just an everyday dress with a what-do-you-call-it over it."

"A pinafore?"

"That's right."

There went my dream portrait in which Liza would look like a very young Gainsborough duchess. But you did not look a gift horse in the mouth, especially one that might bite off your fingers.

"I want her sitting over by that window on a footstool, against those red velvet drapes."

I was beginning to have second thoughts about the whole project. "She's never even been in this room. And she's only a year and a half old. I don't think she will sit still for more than a minute or so."

"She will for me."

Amazingly, she did. When I brought her down to the suitably warm parlor the next morning, John Solum had already set up his easel and propped the blank canvas upon it.

I settled her on the footstool and then retired nervously to an armchair across the room.

After sketching rapidly with a piece of charcoal for perhaps a minute, he said, "Did you ever meet a beaver named Charlie?"

Staring at him with fascinated eyes, Liza shook her head.

"Well, I did. A beaver, you know, is sort of a big rat with a flat tail. This beaver told me he'd always wanted to play drums and cymbals with an orchestra—"

Sketching rapidly, he told how Charlie had practiced by thumping his tail on an empty keg someone had left by the riverbank. Once he had perfected his technique, he had gone to New York, only to be met by one disappointment after another. One orchestra had rejected him because he had no dress suit, another because he had never been to the conservatory. Finally, though, he had persuaded a conductor to give him a chance. His great triumph had been a performance of a new work, *The Battle of Gettysburg*, during which he had played both the snare and kettle drums, pivoting rapidly now and then to strike a cymbal, and, at the appropriate moment, had fired a small cannon by pulling its lanyard with his teeth.

Probably Liza understood little of this. It must have been his appearance in the red knit cap, rather than his narrative, which fascinated her. But anyway she sat there, wide-eyed, for about fifteen minutes. Then he said, "She can go now. I'll work on the background. Bring her down for another few minutes tomorrow, same time."

Four days later, when I had returned Liza to the nursery after her brief sitting, it occurred to me that John Solum, still at work down there, might like some midmorning refreshment. As I entered the parlor and approached him over the thick Axminster, he remained bent over his canvas.

"Would you like a cup of tea?"

He gave a startled yell, and the brush in his hand skidded across the canvas. Whirling around, he hurled the brush, its bristles laden with red paint, to the floor. "Don't ever do that," he shouted, "don't ever do that."

"Just look what you've done to the carpet."

"To hell with your carpet! You're lucky I didn't break this canvas over your head."

I said, reining in my temper, "I can scarcely see you doing that. After all, it's a John R. Solum."

The rage left his face. For the first time I heard him laugh. His laugh had a seldom-used sound, like the creak of a rusty hinge. "Just don't ever startle me," he said. With a rag that hung from one side of the easel, he began to erase the red slash across the skirt of Liza's white pinafore. "Now what do you want?"

"I thought you might like a cup of tea."

He nodded. "Put some rum in it. If you don't have rum, use brandy."

The next day, as he moved toward the front door, carrying case in hand, I said, "Wouldn't you like to look at your portrait of Mrs. Fonsell? It's in the dining room."

"Some other time. Past work doesn't interest me much."

Obviously it did not, because although he came to the house every day for another week, he never once went into the dining room.

The morning he pronounced the portrait finished, he propped it, in the gilt frame he had brought with him, on a table against the parlor wall. "It's good," he said. Then, after a moment: "I'll make a deal with you. You pay only for the frame. But I can exhibit it whenever I choose. I can even take it out of the country if I want to. Fair enough?"

"More than fair."

By the next afternoon Liza's portrait hung in the dining room on the wall opposite the fireplace, gazing with grave blue eyes at the portrait of the beautiful grandmother she had never known.

Chapter 15

EARLY IN MARCH, Jason came home. I was dropping off to sleep that night when I heard his footsteps on the stairs and then along the hall to his room. The sound awoke ambivalent feelings in me. On one hand, there was the softening I had felt toward him ever since, for no matter what reason, he had transferred to me my aunt's interest in Fonsell and Haverly. On the other hand, I felt a return of the outrage that had welled up in me when I first realized that he might have taken Annabelle with him on the *Kestrel*.

That didn't matter, I told myself firmly. All that mattered was whether or not this first voyage had been successful, successful enough to give promise of future security for Liza and me. All that mattered, I thought, smiling into the darkness, was whether or not Jason had brought home the Golden Fleece.

The next morning, stepping from the nursery into the hall, I encountered Jason. He said, "I was coming to see you." He paused. "You're looking well."

"So are you." In fact, he not only looked fit and deeply tanned, but there was a new confidence in his voice, in the set of his shoulders, and in the slight smile that curved his mouth with its full lower lip. "Did you have a pleasant voyage?"

"Very pleasant. How's Liza?"

"She's grown a lot. Would you like to see her? Rose is giving her breakfast."

"Then I'll wait until later. I don't think your Rose likes me much. What I came to ask you is this. Would you like to drive over to the refinery site? On the way I can tell you about the voyage."

"All right. I'll tell Rose, and then get my cloak."

When I descended the front steps a few minutes later, he was waiting beside the buggy. Nora, the dappled mare who shared the stable with the bay saddle horse and aged Toby, stood patiently between the shafts. Jason handed me in. As we drove across the bridge and onto Water Street, the surprised, curious faces of the people who nodded to us reminded me that this was the first time since the day of our return from our wedding journey that Mr. and Mrs. Jason Fonsell had ridden side by side through the village streets.

As we neared Long Wharf he said, "There she is."

The *Kestrel*, her sails furled and her black hull a bit dulled by salt spray and tropic sun, lay alongside the wharf near its landward end. "She needs repainting. And off Nassau we shipped a sea that stove in a hatch cover. That needs more repair. But otherwise it was a highly profitable voyage."

"How profitable?"

His smile was a shade sardonic. "You're your aunt's own niece after all, aren't you? Well, I bought eighteen hundred tons of raw sugar at pretty near my own price. Once it's processed at that New Jersey refinery, it will be worth twice what I paid for it. After deducting the refinery costs, and the expenses of the voyage, I should have a profit of around fifteen thousand dollars."

"Fifteen thousand!"

"Yes, but of course that's not clear profit, not at this stage of the game. The brig is a long way from having paid for itself. And I need more money to build the refinery and buy machinery for it. It may be two or three years before we start showing a profit."

"Yes, I can understand that." But if he just wouldn't insist upon sinking money into a refinery.

We had passed the first of the buildings on Bay Street. He said, reining in, "Here's the site."

I looked at the weed-grown lot, trying to imagine a building there, and the rumble of machinery, and stacks belching smoke into the clean, salty air.

"The foundation will go in next summer," he said. "I've already ordered the machinery. It will be installed before the completion of the building, of course."

I sat silent for a moment, looking across the bay, a steely blue on this cold March morning, to the white column of Cedar Point Lighthouse. Then I said, "Why do you want to build a refinery?"

"Why?" His deeply tanned face looked astonished. "Tell me why not."

"Oh, I don't know. A shipping line is a wonderful idea. This has always been a seagoing town. But maybe your refinery will . . . change things."

"You bet it will. And if you don't like the changes, you'll be about the only one who doesn't. Do you realize this town has been in a depression for almost thirty years, ever since whaling started to decline? Do you know how many enterprises have started up here, only to fail, or at best just get by?" He named some of them. A woolen mill, a stocking factory, a glass factory, an oilcloth factory.

"Yes, I know that."

"If the refinery succeeds, it will mean more than profits for Fonsell and Haverly. It will mean money for every merchant in town, because people will have wages to spend. Not just Sag Harbor people. As the refinery expands, I'll bring in people from the outside."

"Then you're already thinking about expansion?"

"Of course. As Fonsell and Haverly acquires more ships and brings in more sugar, I'll have to expand." He paused. "See all that vacant land up ahead? Plenty of room there for cottages for people who'll work in the refinery. And there's more vacant land on the east side of Rysam Street, and on Burke Street. That will mean more money for the builders."

The prospects he described were pleasant, most people would say. And yet . . . I thought of my aunt's neighbors, the Biemeyers, who had traveled through the mill towns of Massachusetts a few years before. Mrs. Biemeyer had described the rows and rows of sad little cottages, each exactly like its neighbor, and the red brick factories that resembled prisons, pouring smoke from their stacks, and, on the hills above the towns, the brownstone mansions of the mill owners, with iron deer standing on lawns behind high, spike-topped iron picket fences.

Jason said, "Shall we circle back to the bridge by way of Main Street?"

"All right."

He turned the buggy around. We drove through the business district on lower Main Street, where only a few pedestrians, hunched against the cold, moved along the sidewalks, and then past the big frame houses on Captains' Row. If a number of people became rich because of the refinery, would these houses be replaced by the sort Mrs. Biemeyer had described? Would there be forbiddingly tall iron fences where now there were friendly low wooden ones, or no fences at all? I hoped not. Perhaps it meant I had uncultivated tastes, but these houses seemed more beautiful to me than the ones I had seen on Fifth Avenue, and those Mrs. Biemeyer had told me about.

Jason said, "I expect to sail again in about three weeks, if I can get enough cargo together. Part of it is going to be pretty smelly cargo. Hides of Montauk cattle that I'm going to drop off in Jacksonville. It wouldn't be a pleasant trip for passengers. But the next voyage—well, I talked to my father last night, and he wants to go with me."

After a moment he added dryly, "That is, if he can persuade Paul Ronsard to go along with him."

"Dr. Ronsard! Why does your father want him along?"

"Because he's afraid. He wants to see the islands again, but not without the protection of a doctor."

How people could pretend, even to themselves. From Ephraim's disregard of Paul Ronsard's advice, from his jeers at medical men in general and Paul in particular, one would have thought that he was only indulging his doctor by allowing him to call each week. And yet it appeared now that despite his bravado, and his stubborn indulgence in port and brandy, he was a frightened old man who counted upon his doctor's presence to keep him alive, despite his sins.

Well, I would be lonely without Ephraim, and without Paul Ronsard at dinner each Wednesday night.

We had turned off Main Street onto Glover Street now. A few minutes later we crossed the railroad tracks, whose coming to Sag Harbor had awakened yet unrealized hopes of a prosperity rivaling that of the booming thirties and forties. Would Fonsell sugar someday travel these tracks? Or did Jason plan to carry the refinery's products in his own ships?

He said, as we moved along Water Street toward the bridge, "How about you and Liza coming along, voyage after next?"

"To the Caribbean?" I felt a surge of excitement. Often I had thought enviously of the women, including some of my own family, who had lived at a time when fleets of sailing ships linked eastern Long Island with all the world. In those days, captains' wives and children often made the voyages too, so that Hong Kong shops and palm-fringed Caribbean shores became almost as familiar to them as stores along Main Street, or the pebbly beach at Noyack.

I said, "But Liza is still so young."

"She'll be two on June twenty-third." Surprised, I glanced at him. Men usually did not remember such things. "And you could take Rose Murphy with you."

I shook my head. "She gets terribly seasick." Otherwise, she had told me, she would use her savings for a visit to the Old Country. Still, I thought, I would not be afraid to take Liza on the voyage, not with a doctor aboard.

I was silent for a while, and then blurted out, "Was Annabelle Clyssom aboard the *Kestrel?*"

The face he turned toward me held unmistakable astonishment. "No. Whatever made you think she was?"

"I haven't seen her around since before you sailed."

"Oh, I see."

I waited, but apparently that was all he intended to say about her. Had she, I wondered, taken some trip of her own while he was away? If so, it was evident I would not find out about it from him.

I said, "I'll think about going along with you and your father."

"You do that." After a moment he added, "I saw Liza's portrait this morning. My father told me Solum didn't charge for it."

"No. Apparently he indulges himself that way sometimes. If a sitter interests him, as your stepmother and Liza did, he's willing to do a portrait for nothing."

"Well, he's no businessman. If I were in his shoes, able to charge five thousand or more for a portrait—"

"If you were in his shoes," I said, smiling, "you wouldn't be a businessman either."

He shot me a glance. "Do you like men like that? Artists?"

Something in his manner made me feel self-conscious. "I don't know. John Solum's the only artist I ever met."

"Do you like him?"

"I neither like him nor dislike him. I suppose that's because he himself seems to have no feeling for anything except his work. I think people don't exist for him except as portrait subjects."

Jason said nothing, but I could tell that my answer somehow pleased him. Leaning forward, he flicked the mare's haunch with the whip. At a quickened pace, we clattered over the bridge.

Chapter 16

EXCEPT FOR AN overnight trip to the New Jersey refinery, Jason stayed at home for the three weeks the *Kestrel* was in port. At dinner each night I listened with growing fascination while the two men talked of the West Indies, Ephraim reminiscing about the days when pirates mingled with honest seamen on the streets and in the grog shops of Havana, and Jason speaking more prosaically of cane cuttings per annum, and optimum soil and weather conditions for the cultivation of sugar. In particular, he talked of San Isidro, an island which Napoleon had lost to the British shortly after the turn of the century.

"It's about a hundred miles due east of Puerto Rico, and much smaller, of course. But its soil and weather conditions are about the same. Many of the sugar plantations are still owned by Frenchmen. I have a five-year contract with one of them, a man named Aristide d'Auberge."

When the *Kestrel* sailed, Liza accompanied Ephraim and Ruth and me down to the dock. Her eyes filled with wonder as she watched the brig make toward Cedar Point, unfurling its canvas like some giant bird spreading its wings.

Less than a week later, I saw Annabelle Clyssom again.

As I did once each month, I had driven across the bridge that afternoon to air out the Howard Street house. I was opening a kitchen window to the mild April breeze when I heard the knocker strike. Rolling down my sleeves, I moved along the hall and opened the front door.

She stood there on the porch, in the same skirt and tight-waisted jacket she had worn that day, more than two years before, when we had faced each other in a third-floor room of the Fonsell house. Her dark eyes, too, had that same bold, amused look. But there was a new set to her full mouth, and new lines at its corners. Looking past her, I realized how she had known that I was here. I had left the Fonsell buggy and dappled mare beside the hitching post at the curb.

She said, "I'd like to talk to you."

I wanted to refuse her. But the longer she stood there, the more chance there was that one of the Biemeyers might look out a window across the street. I stepped back. "Come in."

I led her through the dust-sheeted parlor to the sitting room, and removed dust covers from two chairs. When we were both seated she looked around her and said, "I should think you'd sell this house. Tramps break into empty houses, you know."

"I'm not afraid of that."

"Houses out on Madison Street have been broken into."

"Those houses are more isolated. Now what did you want to talk about?"

"About your aunt. About her death, I mean."

Wincing inwardly, I wished she were far away, not sitting here in a chair where Aunt Elizabeth often had sat.

"There was a rumor," she said, "that somebody killed her."

The terror and grief I had felt as I knelt beside my aunt's body again washed over me. What I felt must have shown in my face, because she said, in a satisfied tone, "So you thought that too."

I was in control of myself now. "For a little while. My aunt said something which could have indicated that. But Dr. Cantrell told me that stroke victims, when they can speak at all, sometimes say bizarre things. I'm convinced now that her fall was a result of the stroke."

"Are you?"

I said coldly, "Of course. As for the rumor you mentioned, I can't imagine who would have started it. Certainly Dr. Cantrell wouldn't have, or Jason."

"Nobody would have to start it. It would start itself. After all, two violent deaths in the same house—"

She was right about that. I did not reply.

She went on, "Naturally people wondered if the two deaths were connected. I'll bet you wondered about it, right at the first, anyway."

I said sharply, "My aunt's death was two years ago. Why have you come to see me about it now?"

"Well, it's been on my mind all this time. I've kept wanting to tell you that you should go see Jason's mother."

"Jason's mother!"

"Of course. She lived in the Fonsell house, until old Mr. Fonsell threw her out. She might have an idea who killed his wife."

"I doubt that. She hadn't been living in that house for a dozen years when Mrs. Fonsell died." I paused. "But you were there at the time, I believe."

She smiled. "Yes, as the housekeeper. But I didn't kill her, if that thought ever crossed your mind. What reason could I have had?"

Mrs. Burlow had hinted at a reason. What was it? Oh, yes. Mrs. Burlow had insinuated that in those days Annabelle had fixed her eyes, not on Jason, but on his father. In fact, according to Mrs. Burlow, Annabelle had hoped to become the second Mrs. Ephraim Fonsell.

"I mean," Annabelle said, "Mrs. Fonsell and I got along all right. She was always fair with me."

Recollection struck me. "I'd say she was more than fair with you, if she gave you her white jade pendant."

Her eyes narrowed. Then she laughed. "Jason told me about that. You think you saw me wearing it."

"I did see you wearing it, one Sunday when you got off the train." Probably, I realized, she had intended to take off the pendant while still on the train, and place it in the small satchel she had carried. Well, undoubtedly she had remedied that oversight before she reached the Fonsell house.

"The pendant you saw was a fake. I always liked Mrs. Fonsell's—her brother had brought it back from China, she once told me—and so several years ago I drew a sketch of it for a New York jeweler. He copied it in imitation jade and red glass stones. It cost me fifteen dollars." She shrugged. "I have no idea where it is now. As I told Jason, I lost it after I'd had it only a few months."

She was lying. Had Jason realized she was lying? I wanted to say, "If the pendant you wore was a fake, then where is Julia Fonsell's? Her daughter says she knows nothing about it." But Annabelle would reply merely that she had no idea, or perhaps that Julia's widower, financially straitened, had probably sold it. Besides, it was distasteful, wrangling with Annabelle over a dead woman's jewelry, jewelry that neither of us had any right to.

"But to get back to you," she said. "It wouldn't do any harm to go see Jason's mother. She lives in a little village called Green Corners. The railroad will take you within two miles of it." After a moment she added, "She calls herself Mrs. Jackson, Marie Jackson."

"What do you mean, calls herself? She was a widow when Ephraim Fonsell met her. And her husband's name had been Jackson."

Annabelle shrugged. "Maybe that is her right name. Anyway, if you still worry about your aunt's death, why not go see her? I mean, if the two deaths were connected, and she has any additional information about Julia Fonsell's murder—"

Her voice trailed off. When I didn't answer, she got to her feet. "Well, I have things to do."

I too stood up. "Are you still living in Redwood? I haven't seen you for several months."

She looked both surprised and pleased, as if by asking that question I had revealed myself as less knowledgeable than she had supposed. "No. I just came here today to see a friend of mine who works at the Nassau House. I have a little place in Riverhead."

Still fairly nearby, now that we had the railroad. Had Jason provided the "little place"? Or had he broken with her? If so, had she been replaced by someone else? To my dismay, I found I very much wanted to know the answers to those questions. But I would have cut out my tongue before asking.

As I moved with her into the hall, she said, "Well, think about going to see Jason's mother, won't you?"

"There would be no point in thinking. I don't intend to go."

She shrugged. "Suit yourself. But in your place, I'd go."

As soon as the door had closed behind her, I moved to the parlor window, and watched until she disappeared in the direction of Main Street. He must have broken with her, I decided. And so it must have been malice which had prompted her visit. She wanted to reawaken painful doubts in me. Also, perhaps, she had hoped to annoy or embarrass Jason, in some way I could not fathom, by inducing me to visit his mother. Well, I would forget the whole episode.

I did not, of course. No matter what Annabelle's motive in making the suggestion, the fact remained that Jason's mother might indeed be able to throw some light upon Julia Fonsell's death. And although I had tried resolutely to do so, I could not escape the thought that my aunt, that last afternoon of her life, had acquired some knowledge about that same death.

And so, one morning in late May, I succumbed to temptation. Leaving Liza in Rose Murphy's care, I took the train to a station about a third of the way to New York. The aged driver of the lone hackney cab drawn up at the platform said that of course he knew where Green Corners was.

"Do you know where a Mrs. Jackson lives, Marie Jackson?"

"Oh, sure. She's been there maybe twenty years now."

We drove along a road flanked by dark green fields of potatoes, and then through a hamlet so small that one frame building housed the post office, general store, and Justice of the Peace. We stopped before a white frame cottage, set back on a neat lawn. Late-blooming yellow tulips bordered the brick walk. I asked the driver, "Will you wait for me? I won't be long."

"Take your time."

On this warm day the front door stood open. I knocked on the screen's edge. A woman emerged from the doorway at the end of a short hall and moved toward me. She said, surprised pleasure in her voice, "Why, you must be Irene! Come in, honey, come in."

She opened the screen door wide. I saw that she was plump and gray-haired and snub-nosed. Probably she had never been handsome, not even in her youth. But her face held an almost childlike openness that I found attractive. She led me halfway down the hall and then into a small parlor where every available surface—backs and arms of horsehair chairs and sofas, small tables, even the fireplace mantel—was covered with rectangles and oblongs of pink tatting.

When we were seated I said, "How is it you knew me?"

"Jason told me how you look." So apparently he did visit her. She went on, smiling, "Tell me, does my granddaughter look like you?"

Her granddaughter. So Jason had not told her the circumstances of our marriage. "I suppose so. At least her hair is dark and curly." I paused, and then asked, "Let's see. Did Jason visit you the last time he was home?"

"He was here twice. He's always been good about visiting me. Irene, do you mind if I tat?"

"Of course not."

She reached into a work basket beside her chair. Seconds later, hands busy with pink thread and shuttle, she asked, "How is Ephraim?"

Her tone was so matter-of-fact, so devoid of anything resembling bitterness, that surprise held me speechless for a moment. Then I said, "He seems fairly well."

"Still drinking, I guess."

"I'm afraid so."

She sighed. "He don't pay attention to anyone. He never did."

Puzzled, I looked at the plain face which seemed to hold nothing except mingled concern and resignation. She went on, "Jason tells me Ephraim didn't drink at table when your aunt was there. She might have been a good influence on him, if she'd been spared long enough." Her light-blue eyes looked up from her shuttle. "I was sure sorry to hear she'd passed on."

"Thank you."

"She was a little bit of a thing, Jason said. That kind usually lives to be a hundred."

For a few seconds we sat in silence. Then I said, "I know I have no right to ask this. But don't you feel any resentment toward—toward your—"

"Toward Ephraim?" Like her voice, the eyes she raised to me were calm. "Why, Irene, he played fair with me. He never once told me he loved me, not even at the first. And when he came back to San Francisco, and saw Jason—well, he played more than fair with me. He brought both of us back to Long Island with him."

"But later on—"

"You mean when he told me I had to leave? I'd always

known that would probably happen, someday. He'd told me so."

"But didn't you miss your son?"

"Of course. I missed him something awful. But Ephraim wanted him there. And by the time a boy's six or seven, he needs his father as much as his mother, maybe more."

The shuttle flew in and out through the loops in the pink thread. She went on, her tone brightening, "Sometimes I thought maybe I was wrong about that. But I wasn't. Jason turned out real fine."

"Yes," I said, hoping she didn't hear the reserved note in my voice.

"You mustn't feel sorry for me, Irene. Thanks to Ephraim, I've lived in comfort all these years. Oh, I used to work out, but only because I got lonesome sitting here, not because I had to."

"Work out?"

"I did housework for folks here on the island. And for about two years I worked for a New York couple who spent their summers out here." She sighed. "I'd still like to work, but Jason gets too upset. You see, he's always trying to give me money. What do I need with more money? But if I try to work, he feels that proves I'm in need." She shook her head. "Stubborn as a mule, just like his father."

"Yes," I said again, in what I hoped was a neutral tone.

Out in the street, the thin old cab horse shook his harness. Mrs. Jackson said, turning to look through the screen, "Why, the cab's still there. He'll charge waiting time, you know."

"That's all right."

She smiled, and took up her tatting. "I guess it is. You and Jason will be rich someday soon."

"I know he wants to be rich."

"He will be."

After a moment I said hesitantly, "Perhaps I shouldn't ask this, but did you know Julia Fonsell?"

135

She seemed surprised by my question. "Oh, yes. A few months after Ephraim married her, Jason came down with scarlet fever. He was seven then. Ephraim fetched me, and I stayed there four days, until the crisis passed. His wife was expecting her first then. She was awfully nice to me. Maybe it sounds strange, but we were just two women, both of us scared, me over Jason, and her over having her first baby."

"Did you ever see her again?"

"Once, years later. It must have been only a few weeks before she died. I was in New York then, cooking for that couple I told you about. One afternoon on Fourteenth Street I saw her come out of a hotel. There was a man with her. He put her in a hansom cab, tipped his hat, and walked away."

A hotel? On Fourteenth Street? But John Solum had told me Julia stayed with a relative, some woman who gave singing lessons, and who lived south of Washington Square. Then I realized that she could have been calling on someone at the hotel, or having lunch there.

"Did you recognize the man?"

"Oh, no. I'd never seen him before. I don't even remember what he looked like."

He could have been anyone, I realized. John Solum, or some friend of the woman she was staying with. He might even have been some polite stranger who had opened the hotel door for her, and then handed her into a waiting cab.

"I always felt so sorry for her," Mrs. Jackson said.

"For Julia Fonsell?" Sorry for the woman who had supplanted her? I looked at the round, snub-nosed face, but could see no hint of irony.

"Of course. She had a terrible life. Did Ephraim ever tell you her father and brother went to prison?" I nodded. "Imagine growing up with a thing like that. My folks were poor, but none of them ever went to prison."

She drew a series of tatted loops into a circle, wound the

thread around the fingers of her left hand, and plied the shuttle with her right. "And then that accident her first child had. Jason tells me Ruth's still not right in the head. And then, of course, that last terrible thing that happened to her."

After a moment she added, "Well, at least she was spared one thing. She never knew her son drowned."

For a piercing moment I again stood beside a yellow-haired boy, with his hand lying warm over mine on the ship's rail as we looked down at the glassy, foam-flecked wake. Then I thrust the memory away.

"Have you ever wondered who killed Julia Fonsell?"

"Why, of course not!" Her tone was emphatic, but for the first time I saw something guarded in her face. "An escaped lunatic killed her. Didn't you know that? No, maybe you didn't. I guess you were only a tiny girl then."

"No, I was ten. I heard about the lunatic. But . . ." My voice trailed off.

"I know." Suddenly her face flushed, and tears sprang to her round, pale blue eyes. "You heard folks say maybe Ephraim did it. Some even said Jason, although he wasn't much more than a boy then."

"I'm sorry. I shouldn't have mentioned it." I wanted to add that I had done so only because of the circumstances of my aunt's death. But I could not say that now. Obviously I had distressed her enough already.

"That's all right," she said, but her voice still shook. "It was just so awful, having folks say that about Ephraim, and even about my own boy—"

"I'm really awfully sorry."

"Well, we don't have to talk about it." She smiled at me, and then leaned over to place her tatting in her work basket. "Now I'll make us a nice cup of tea."

"I'm afraid I'll have to get back to the station."

"But you just got here!"

"I mustn't miss my train."

"No, I suppose not."

As we moved toward the hallway, she said, "Will you bring my granddaughter to see me, real soon?"

Not knowing what else to answer, I said, "I'll try." Hand on the screen door, I turned impulsively and added, "I'm sorry you weren't at your son's—at our wedding." I had never thought of it before, but now it struck me how forlorn she must have felt, knowing that thirty miles away her only child was being married.

She said wonderingly, "Why, Irene! You think I'd of wanted to come? Enough folks remember Jason's father was never married to me. No point in reminding them."

Chapter 17

AS THE TRAIN carried me east through the green countryside, I reflected with chagrin that I had allowed Annabelle Clyssom to send me on a wild-goose chase. From Jason's mother I had gained one tiny, useless bit of information—that almost a dozen years ago, Julia Fonsell had emerged from a New York hotel and been handed into a cab by a man who might have been anyone.

Did Mrs. Jackson know anything else, something of importance which she had withheld from me? Remembering the round, guileless face, I doubted that she had. Nor did I think Annabelle had believed Mrs. Jackson could tell me anything. Annabelle had been motivated solely by a desire to make mischief.

About three weeks later I came downstairs one morning to find Jason as well as his father and Ruth in the dining room. Turning from the covered dishes on the sideboard, a plate heaped with sausages and scrambled eggs in his hand, he smiled at me and said, "I wondered when you'd be down."

There was no need to ask whether or not the *Kestrel's* second voyage had been a success. Even more so than after his first return from the Caribbean, his deeply tanned face radiated confidence. Nevertheless, as I spooned scrambled eggs onto a plate, I asked, "Good voyage?"

"Excellent. And the next one should be even better."

After breakfast he returned to the brig to supervise the discharge of its cargo, a deckload of farm machinery which he had picked up in Wilmington on the homeward voyage. But that afternoon we drove to the refinery site. As the buggy carried us across the bridge, I knew that I should say, "I went to see your mother while you were gone." But in the days since my visit to Green Corners I had grown apprehensive. How would he react to the news that, without consulting him, I had called upon his mother? After all, he had never evinced interest in bringing the two of us together. In fact, he had never mentioned her to me. And so, as we moved off the bridge onto Water Street, and followed its curving course toward Long Wharf, I said nothing. Instead I listened to his account of the huge new coppers—boiling vats for sugar cane—which Aristide d'Auberge had installed on his San Isidro plantation.

When we reached the refinery site, I saw that the excavation for the cellar was much larger than it had been only days before, when a shopping expedition had brought me across the bridge. The foreman of the pick-and-shovel-wielding workmen was Carl Johansen, a blond giant who made a varied livelihood as a fisherman, harvest hand, and day laborer. As Jason and I walked from the buggy toward him, Carl leaned on his shovel and said, "Hello, Mr. Fonsell. Everything going just fine here."

"I can see it is." Jason turned to me, smiling. "A year from now I won't be unloading raw sugar in New Jersey. I'll bring it here."

The three of us chatted for a few minutes. Then Jason and I returned to the buggy. When he had handed me up onto the seat he said, "Wait a moment. There's something I forgot to tell Carl."

As I watched the two men talk, I saw Mr. Thomas Hiram moving stiffly toward them, aided by his cane. Mr. Hiram was almost eighty, a church vestryman, and one of the few former whaleship owners who was as well off now as he was thirty years before. He had invested his share of the million-dollar whale harvest of 1847, not in more whaling ventures, but in bank stocks, and, later on, railroad stocks. He was also one of the men who had refused to back Jason.

He halted beside the other two men and said, in his cracked old voice, "Going to get rich, are you?"

Even from fifteen yards away, I could see the flush mount in Jason's dark face. His voice, though, was even. "I hope to make a few dollars."

"Well, I'm sure glad none of my money is sunk in all this."

I saw Jason's flush deepen. There had been contempt in the old voice. Contempt for the upstart, the bastard son of a confirmed rounder and the illiterate daughter of a San Francisco tavern keeper. To my amazement, I felt a surge of protective anger.

Mr. Hiram was moving toward me now. He said, "Afternoon, Irene. How are you?"

There was only a hint of reserve in his manner now. After all, no matter how much the town speculated about my hasty marriage, or even the paternity of my child, I was not an outsider. I was the niece of Elizabeth Haverly, and the daughter of Captain James Haverly, who had died in the Union cause.

His change of manner, instead of mollifying me, only inflamed my resentment. I said shortly, "I'm well, thank you."

"And your little girl?"

"She's well too."

He sighed. "I often think of your aunt. A fine woman. She's greatly missed, greatly missed." I nodded, and then waited grimly for him to add, "It's a pity to see her substance wasted on a foolish enterprise." Fortunately, he did not. He said, "Well, good day to you," tipped his old-fashioned beaver stovepipe, and hobbled off toward Main Street.

A few minutes later Jason got into the buggy beside me and gathered up the reins. As we moved past Long Wharf, I said, "I hope you didn't allow Mr. Hiram to bother you."

"I didn't," he said, but a muscle along his jaw was jumping. "He'll sing a different tune someday, he and a lot of others."

I did not answer. Should I tell him about my visit to his mother now? No, I decided. Not on his first day home, and not when he was already upset by that encounter with Mr. Hiram.

After we had crossed the bridge, Jason asked, "Have you decided about you and Liza coming on the next voyage?"

"Yes, I'd like to. Rose says she'll go back to the Biemeyers while we're away."

The smile he gave me warmed his whole face. "That's fine."

Late the next afternoon I learned how much wiser I would have been to tell him about my visit to Green Corners.

That morning, after I came down to breakfast, I found that Jason had already left the house. He did not return for lunch. But in the late afternoon, as I knelt in the walled garden, snipping stalks of iris that had finished blooming, I heard his rapid footsteps in the lower hall. He pushed the screen door back and walked over to stand above me. "So you went to see my mother."

Nerves tightening apprehensively, I looked up into his grim face. Then, laying the shears aside, I got to my feet. "Why shouldn't I have gone to see her?"

"That isn't the question. Why did you?"

"I don't see that there's anything so wrong in—"

"Then I'll tell you what's wrong! I don't want her upset. She's had enough trouble in her life. She's entitled to whatever peace—"

"Did she say I'd upset her?"

"No! But I could tell you had."

"On the whole, I thought she enjoyed my visit. She said she had."

"Of course," he said bitterly. "She's so straightforward herself that she never questions other people's motives. She seemed to think you came there merely because you wanted to meet her. But I know that wasn't so. You didn't just take it into your head, after all this time, to go see my mother. Now what was your reason?"

Anger set me to trembling. "Annabelle Clyssom was the reason."

"Annabelle!"

"Yes!" I told him of my conversation with her in the Howard Street house.

"And you took her advice?" His voice rose. "Just on her say-so, you went to Green Corners, and questioned my mother about something that happened years ago, something she had nothing to do with?"

"I didn't think she had anything to do with Julia Fonsell's death." My voice too had become loud. "I just thought she might know something about it."

"How could she know anything? She was living thirty miles away, a good day's travel in those days. She hadn't even been in the Harbor for many years before that. So how could she—"

"As a matter of fact," I said icily, "your mother did tell me something that happened only a few weeks before Mrs. Fonsell's death."

I saw surprised apprehension in his eyes. For himself? His father or mother? He asked, "What did she tell you?"

"She saw Julia Fonsell in New York, coming out of a hotel on Fourteenth Street." Even as I spoke, I wished I had not let him anger me to the point of repeating that meager bit of information.

"And?"

"There was a man with her. He put Mrs. Fonsell into a carriage."

Perhaps two seconds passed before Jason asked, "What man?"

"Your mother didn't know him."

"And that's all?"

"Well, yes."

I saw relief in his face, and then rekindled anger. "And to get that priceless bit of knowledge you went to my mother, raked up the past, forced her to remember that some people believe my father beat my stepmother to death—or that I did. Can you realize how much my mother suffered over those rumors?"

Remembering the indignant pain in Mrs. Jackson's plain, childlike face, I felt a stab of guilt. But as often happens, guilt only increased my defensive anger.

He said, "What are you going to do with your important revelation? Go to New York? Ask at Fourteenth Street hotels if anyone remembers who handed Julia Fonsell into a carriage that day?"

"Maybe I will," I said. "Maybe someone ought to."

"And you're that someone." Again his voice rose. "What the hell business is it of yours, anyway?"

I cried, "I'll tell you why it's my business! Julia Fonsell wasn't the only one to die in this house. My aunt died here."

He eyed me somberly. "So we're back to that, are we?"

"Yes, we're back to that."

Feeling suddenly bleak, I knew that we would always come back to that. Always in some part of my mind—and perhaps in his—my aunt's crumpled body would be lying in the hall, and I would be looking up at him with cold surmise.

He said, "Under the circumstances, perhaps it would be best if you didn't entrust yourself and Liza to my care. On the *Kestrel*, I mean."

So I would not see that lush little island set in an iridescent sea. Instead, as late summer passed into gray November, Liza and I would still be here in this tragedy-haunted house, with only Ruth and Mrs. Burlow and Rose for company. "Yes, I'd rather stay here."

"Fine," he said in a constricted voice. "But don't go to Green Corners. Just don't bother my mother, ever again." Without waiting for my answer, he opened the wooden gate. I heard his footsteps crunching over the gravel path that led to the stables.

After a moment I picked up my shears and, leaving the severed iris stalks where they lay, moved slowly into the house. As I placed the shears on a shelf just inside the back door, I heard Ruth and Mrs. Burlow in the kitchen, talking in loud, self-conscious tones. They must have stood at the kitchen window which opened onto the garden, I realized now, listening to every word Jason and I had said.

I moved down the hall, now filled with evening shadows. "Irene."

Turning, I saw Ephraim in the doorway of his den. Even in this dim light, I could see that he looked older and more tired than he had at lunch that day. I said, "So you heard."

"The way you two shouted, maybe they heard you over on Main Street." He sighed. "It's too bad. I wanted you and Liza to come along with us. I was even hoping that you and Jason . . ."

The sentence trailed off. From the pang his words brought me, I realized that I must have been entertaining, at least unconsciously, that same hope. "It was never anything more than—an arrangement," I said, and turned toward the stairs. As I climbed, I heard the buggy roll rapidly along the gravel drive beside the house.

Jason did not return that night, nor on the following day, a Wednesday. Whether he was aboard the *Kestrel* or in New York, or with his mother, or at Annabelle's "little place," I did not know. Nor if I had any sense, I told myself, would I care.

As usual on Wednesday night, Paul Ronsard joined us

for dinner. And as usual, his presence had a tonic effect on Ephraim. The night before, with his son absent, the old man had sat tired and silent at dinner. But now Paul soon led him to reminisce about the exotic trees—Australian gum trees, Caribbean mahogany, Mediterranean cedars—which he and other sea captains had brought home with them and planted, with varying success, along Sag Harbor streets. No wonder, I thought, that Ephraim was in fact so dependent upon the man he publicly derided.

The next morning I woke to leaden skies and a strong east wind. Nevertheless, as I descended the stairs, I planned to carry out my original intention of going over to the Howard Street house that day. Empty houses, I had discovered these past two years, need not only regular airing, but sweeping and dusting, as well as inspection for the presence of mice, chipmunks, and squirrels.

But just as I was about to walk back to the carriage house, rain began to fall, first in scattered drops that made almost dollar-sized splotches on the garden's flagstone walk, and then in a steady downpour. It was scarcely a day, I decided, to air out a house. I went back upstairs, changed to my oldest calico, and descended to the kitchen, which was filled with steam redolent of the strawberries Mrs. Burlow was putting up. All that morning and for two hours after lunch I worked beside her, stemming and washing berries, and fishing jars out of the big kettle of boiling water. Then, around three-thirty, the rain stopped, and a few minutes later watery sunlight broke through the clouds. I said, rolling down my sleeves, "I think I'll go over to Howard Street."

"This late?"

"I can still spend a couple of hours cleaning."

"The wind's still easterly. The rain may not be over."

"I'll take the chance."

Twenty minutes later I led old Toby from his stall through the wide doorway into the carriage house. As I backed him between the shafts of Aunt Elizabeth's surrey, I wondered where the buggy and the dappled mare were. Probably they were at the livery stable near the depot. That was where Jason would have left them if he had taken the train to Annabelle's "little place" in Riverhead, or to his mother's house, or on to New York.

As I approached the bridge I saw that John Solum too had taken a chance that the rain was over. He stood down there on the cove's narrow beach, only his shoulders and his head, covered by a black sou'wester, visible above his easel. He looked up as Toby's hoofs struck the bridge. I waved, and he lifted the hand that held his brush in a brief salute.

When I reached the Howard Street house I did not leave Toby tied to the hitching post at the curb. Instead I drove back to the stable, unharnessed him, and led him to a stall. It might start raining hard again, and a horse of almost nineteen could contract pneumonia if left standing in a downpour.

After I had unlocked the back door, I took a broom, dustpan, and dustcloth from the broom closet, put on the apron hanging there, and then walked along the hall to the foot of the stairs. Hand on the newel post, I glanced across the hall and through the parlor's open doorway.

Something was wrong in there. Something had changed from the way I had left it.

Before I had even crossed the parlor threshold, I realized what had caught my attention. Always during my visits to this empty house I looked under dust covers to make sure that no field mouse had gnawed its way through fabric to make a nest in a down cushion or an upholstered chair seat. When replacing a dust cover I was always careful to see that it touched the floor on all sides. But now the cover on the long red velvet sofa was askew, revealing the carved mahogany legs at one end. Had I failed to cover the sofa properly? After all, during my last visit to this house, I had been upset by Annabelle's unexpected arrival.

I lifted the dust cover. The down-filled velvet cushions had been flattened, as if by the pressure of a body stretched out at full length. I might have failed to adjust the dust cover properly. But I would not have failed to plump up the cushions. I was sure of it.

A tramp, I thought. Annabelle had spoken of tramps breaking into empty houses. But I had thought that no tramp would choose this house, flanked as it was by houses not more than fifty yards away, and faced by the Biemeyers' house across the street.

I stood there, looking down at those crushed cushions, and aware now of the utter silence. When Aunt Elizabeth and I had lived here, there had always been some sound, if only the ticking of the tall clock in the hall, or the pretty French traveling clock, glass-sided and gilt-framed, on the parlor fireplace mantel . . .

My gaze flew to the mantel. Yes, the clock was still there. What was more, other small but fairly valuable ornaments, such as the Dresden shepherdess on a marble-topped table by the window, were still in place. Surely a tramp who had surreptitiously entered this house—through a rear window, or the coal chute—would not scruple to stuff that figure into his pocket, or that domed glass paperweight which, when shaken, released an artificial snowstorm on the occupants of the tiny sleigh in its transparent depths.

And a tramp would not have been content with just a night's shelter. He would have seized the chance to prepare a warm meal.

I hurried back to the kitchen. I lifted stove lids. No ashes clung to the grate's iron ribs. I looked at the sink. Its tin lining was unstained, and the mouth of the hand pump beside it was dry. Obviously no one had prepared a meal here.

And so I must have been responsible for those crushed

sofa cushions. I recalled then that after Annabelle's departure I had busied myself with not strictly necessary tasks, trying to escape the painful doubts she had reawakened in me. At one point I had placed books from the parlor's glass-fronted case on the muslin-shrouded sofa, dusted them, and returned them to their shelves. Upset as I was, I must have neglected to plump up the cushions afterward, and to adjust the dust cover.

Moving back to the foot of the stairs, I picked up my cleaning equipment and climbed to the third floor. In my grandfather's time, when a family of seven plus several servants had lived in this house, the third floor bedrooms had been occupied. But during my years here they had stood vacant. At the end of the hall I propped my broom and dustpan against the wall, opened a door, and climbed bare stairs to the attic.

The gray light coming through the small window set only a foot above the floor was faint. With a match from my apron pocket, I lit the lantern that hung by a hook from the steeply slanted ceiling. I was shaking out the match when the first drops of returning rain pattered on the roof. Seconds later, it became a steady roar. As long as rain fell with such violence, I would have to stay here. I could not force poor old Toby to slog through deep mud and blinding rain. No one at the Fonsell house would worry. They all knew where I had gone.

Carrying the lantern, I looked in corners, and behind old trunks and wooden boxes and barrels. No trace of a rodent invasion. I was about to blow out the lantern, preparatory to descending the attic stairs, when I thought better of it. By now, with rain and heavy clouds blotting out most of the remaining daylight, I might find the lower floor quite dark. The lantern in hand, I descended the steps. The third floor hall was dark indeed, its window at the far end only a gray-black rectangle. I opened doors and, holding the lantern high, looked at bare old bureaus, and beds stripped even of their mattresses. Each room was dusty, but I would not bother about that today. After sweeping the hall I would descend to the lower floors, and dust the more valuable pieces of furniture.

Placing the lantern on the hall floor, I began to sweep. I moved swiftly, wanting to finish the task. I found myself disturbed by the rain's roar, so unbroken that it was like a kind of silence, and by the thought of these rooms that had stood empty since before I was born, and by my own grotesquely tall shadow which, as I moved about, was cast now on the hall runner, and now on a closed door, and now on the ceiling. Once, seeing a dim figure standing at the end of the hall, I gave a smothered cry—and then realized it was my own reflection in a windowpane that had turned inky black.

At last I emptied the dustpan into a small metal bin, which I kept for that purpose near the attic door. Awkwardly grasping the broom and dustpan handles in my left hand, and the lantern in my right, I moved toward the head of the stairs. Then, my heart jumping, I stopped short.

From the floor below had come a muffled sound, as if someone, moving in the dark, had collided with a wall, or a piece of furniture.

Someone was in the house. Someone must have been here all along, following my movements by their sound, perhaps even looking at me when I passed some hidden vantage point. I could imagine him standing in the open doorway of some room on the dark second floor, eyes fixed on my lantern-cast shadow on the stairs.

Who was down there? A harmless tramp? If so, why hadn't he taken advantage of the rain and darkness to slip out the unlocked back door? No, it was someone else. Someone who knew I was coming here today. Someone who, as I wielded broom and dustpan, had been waiting for—what? The courage to carry out the intention that had brought him here?

I still had not moved. Only my blood moved, pounding in my ears so loudly that I could hear it through the rain's roar. Think, I commanded myself, try to think. Dart into one of these empty rooms up here, push a bureau against the door, and then open a window and scream? No, that skulker in the blackness down there knew that now I was aware of his presence. The paralyzed immobility of my shadow must have told him. Before I could barricade myself into one of these rooms, he would be up the stairs and bursting in upon me.

Get out. Just get out of the house. Blow the lantern out, and then try to run past him through the darkness. I lifted the lantern, opened its glass door, blew. I set the lantern on the carpet. Then, through blackness broken only by the lantern's afterimage swimming before my eyes, I plunged down the stairs. No hand reached out to grasp me as I turned at the newel post. Moving almost as surely along this familiar hall as if I could see, I raced toward the stairs leading to the front door and safety.

Movement behind me, through a yawning doorway, movement I sensed rather than heard. I was able to let out one high scream. Then something crashed down upon my head. I knew blinding pain, and then blankness.

My head throbbed, more excruciatingly than ever in my life before. Light struck through my closed eyelids, adding to the pain. And someone was sprinkling cold liquid on my face.

Reluctantly I opened my eyes. Rose Murphy knelt beside me, her round face taut with anxiety in the light from the oil lamp on the floor. She said, on an expelled breath, "That's better, love, that's better." Puzzled, I looked up at her, aware that I lay in the second floor hall of my aunt's house, but not knowing, in that first moment, how I happened to be there. I tried to sit up.

She said, "No, better not." Then, as I lay back: "Who did that to you? Who hit you with that thing?"

Following the direction of her gaze, I turned my throbbing head. There on the hall runner lay a heavy brass poker. About a third of the way up its length there was a partially dried stain, dark red and glistening in the lamplight.

I said, with an effort, "I don't know. Someone—"

Someone had struck me down, I thought, a coldness in the pit of my stomach now, just as someone had struck Julia Fonsell down. But her assailant had struck blow after blow, until he was sure she would never move or speak again.

I remembered the scream ripping from my throat. Was that why, unlike Julia Fonsell, I had been left alive? Had he fled into the rainy night, afraid that despite the storm's up-roar someone had heard that scream?

The rain. I said, "The rain's stopped."

"Yes, it stopped over an hour ago. You didn't come back, so I got worried. But there's nothing to worry about now, love. I went across to the Biemeyers. Mr. Biemeyer's gone to fetch the doctor, and his son's gone to fetch Jason."

Jason. Just the day before yesterday, I had quarreled with Jason. "No," I said.

Rose said, not understanding, "Oh, he's home. He drove in not half an hour ago. I went out to the carriage house and told him not to unhitch, because I wanted to drive the buggy over here."

Jason, I thought again. I had told him angrily that perhaps I *would* go to hotels along New York's Fourteenth Street and—

"It must have been a tramp," Rose said. "Some dirty old tramp."

No, not a tramp. Jason, or someone else. Someone else who knew I still had these tormenting doubts that my aunt's death had no relation to Julia Fonsell's. Someone who was afraid of me.

I heard the front door open and close, and then Dr. Cantrell's heavy tread upon the stairs. A moment later he knelt beside me. "Rose, get a pillow for her head, and then bring me a basin of warm water." Looking down at me, he went on, "I don't think it's too bad, but I'd rather not move you until I've bathed the wound and bandaged it."

"Jason—"

"He'll be here. Mr. Biemeyer said he'd sent his son to fetch him. Funny thing, I parted with Jason at the depot not forty minutes ago. We rode out from New York on the train together."

Forty minutes ago. But the rain had stopped over an hour ago. Rose had said. And so, while I fled through the rain-loud blackness along this hall, Jason had been seated beside Dr. Cantrell on a Sag Harbor-bound train.

Rose slipped a pillow under my head and then went down to the kitchen. Soon I heard the front door open and close, and footsteps ascend the stairs.

Jason said, dropping to one knee, "For God sake, what happened?" His dark brows were drawn together until they made an almost continuous line.

"Jason," I said, "Jason—"

After a moment he said, in a completely neutral tone, "Yes?"

"I'm afraid. Don't leave us here. Take Liza and me to San Isidro with you."

Still in that neutral tone, Jason said, "If you like."

Chapter 18

STANDING BESIDE THE *Kestrel*'s rail, I looked across shimmering water at the island of San Isidro. "It's the cone of an extinct volcano," Jason had said one night at dinner in the Fonsell house. "Of course, it hasn't been a volcano for millions of years. Earth has washed down to form a small coastal plain, and on the side facing the Caribbean the volcanic core has eroded away entirely. But you can still make out the shape of the cone."

I could. From this far away the island looked like a jaggedly broken cup, afloat on its broken saucer in the opalescent sea. But the cup was not emerald green, as Jason had described it. By some trick of the late afternoon light, the jungle-clad mountains which encircled the central plain looked blue, a velvety soft blue, deeper than the blue tropic sky. On the portion of the island facing us, where the cone had worn away to sea level, I could see a wharf, with two three-masted schooners alongside it, running back to a palm-fringed, pinkish beach. On upward-sloping land beyond the beach, buildings—yellow and pink and white and green—rose on three sides of a dazzling white plaza.

It looked beautiful, idyllically beautiful, like the Peaceable Kingdom of prophecy where all creatures will live in gentle harmony. But that, I knew, was illusion. On those velvety blue jungle slopes countless tiny tragedies no doubt were being enacted right at that moment. The wild pig screamed as the snake's fangs sunk deep. The turquoise butterfly was slashed to shreds by a bird's voracious beak. A mahogany tree, strangled at last by the thick vines wound around it, crashed to the underbrush.

And, thanks to books Paul Ronsard had brought along on the voyage, I knew that the island's human history had been far from peaceful. In the sixteenth century Spanish galleons had anchored in that natural harbor just ahead, and armor-clad soldiers, pantalooned seamen, and gentlemen in doublet and hose had rowed ashore, where small, copper-skinned natives, awed but friendly, had waited to welcome them. Less than two generations later, the copper-skinned men and women had vanished, wiped out by the brutalities of slavery, and by European diseases. In the eighteenth century the island, its sugar and coffee plantations now manned by African slaves, had passed to the French as part of the settlement of the Seven Years' War.

Early in the nineteenth century, the British had seized the island from Napoleon. But almost as soon as the British fleet, leaving English administrators in charge, had departed, the slave revolt in Haiti had spread to San Isidro. Plantation houses in the interior had been burned, and their occupants slaughtered. And before the returning British warships could land forces to put down the revolt, the blacks had set fire to every building in the harbor, and then fought the invading British, so that the limestone-paved plaza up ahead was slippery not only with blood, but with black, liquid sugar from the burning warehouses. The British had prevailed finally, the town had been rebuilt, and the surviving blacks re-enslaved—until, a half dozen years later, England had outlawed slavery in all its possessions.

I could hear Jason's voice from the quarterdeck now. A few seconds later crew members began to swarm up the ratlines and along the yards, taking in sail. It was time to arouse my daughter from her nap, and pack our possessions. Turning, I descended the companionway.

Half an hour later someone knocked on the door of the

cabin Liza and I shared. Pulse quickening, I closed the valise I had been packing and moved to answer the knock. It must be Jason, come to take us ashore. I had seen little of him during the voyage—actually less, in fact, than during the days before the *Kestrel* sailed, when he had remained away from home most of the time. Aboard ship he had kept to his cabin and the quarterdeck. At mealtimes in the dining salon, he and his father and Dr. Ronsard had sat at one of the two tables, leaving Liza and me to share a table with whichever of the ship's officers were not on watch. But surely now . . .

I opened the door. A thin, eyeglassed man I had never seen before asked pleasantly, "Mrs. Fonsell?" His accent was British. "My name is Claude Smythe. I'm your husband's business agent here on the island. He has asked me to escort you and your father-in-law and Dr. Ronsard ashore."

"Thank you. Are we all to stay at the hotel?"

"The elder Mr. Fonsell and Dr. Ronsard will. I engaged rooms for them near the room Captain Fonsell usually occupies when he's ashore. But because of the little girl, Captain Fonsell thought you might be more comfortable in separate quarters."

I said, in flat voice, "I see."

"You have a small rented house, with everything laid on. I took the liberty of engaging both a general servant and a nursemaid for your stay. They have both worked for my wife and me, and so I can vouch for their capabilities."

"That was very kind of you."

"Not at all. I'll wait out here until you are ready."

A few minutes later, holding Liza's hand, I followed Mr. Smythe down the gangplank. He carried both of the valises I had packed. My trunk would be brought ashore the next day.

On the wharf, Ephraim and Paul Ronsard were already seated, backs to the driver, in an open carriage. As I approached it, I turned to look up at the brig's quarterdeck.

Jason was not there. Mr. Smythe handed me into the carriage, lifted Liza onto my lap, and got in beside me.

As the carriage rattled over the wharf's planks, Paul smiled at me and said, "Well, here we are, in Blackbeard territory." He turned to the agent. "San Isidro was a pirate hideaway at one time, wasn't it?"

"Oh, most assuredly. Early in the century the place swarmed with cutthroats. Of course, around 1825, you Americans got together with us and cleaned the last of them out of the Caribbean. But people walking along the beaches sometimes find pirate gold even now, dollars or guilders or sovereigns."

Paul said, "We'll keep that in mind, won't we, Irene? Perhaps while we're gathering those rare shells we read about, we'll make our fortune."

Gratefully, I returned his smile. Without him, the voyage would have been tedious. Jason seemed always busy, and Ephraim, complaining of rheumatism and an upset stomach, had kept to his cabin most of the time. But Paul had often strolled along the deck with me, talking of Caribbean history, and of the visit he would make to the hospital on the Atlantic side of San Isidro. "That's the way I justified it to myself—turning over my patients to a colleague, I mean, so that I could make this trip. I'll do some research into tropical diseases. And please don't ask me how many cases of yaws or leprosy I expect to treat on Long Island."

"I won't ask you," I said. "I'm just glad you did come."

We were moving across the plaza now. Ephraim sat silent, head sunk low in his collar. He turned it now and then to look at the pastel buildings with their second-story balconies, and their jutting roofs that shadowed the sidewalks. I knew he had never been to San Isidro. But his face held a wryly reminiscent look, as if he were thinking of other palm-fringed islands, other shadowed sidewalks where, as along these sidewalks, graceful women with complexions like pale brown satin had walked with bundles balanced on their white-turbaned heads. By contrast, Liza was voluble. She had become fluent of late in a language which sometimes even I was hard put to understand. "Ooh, pity, pity," she kept saying, twisting about on my lap, "pity gween howze, pity broo howze." Pointing a dimpled finger at a bundle-carrying woman, she asked, "Weddy ith bebul?"

"No," I said, "the lady doesn't have a baby in that bundle." I looked at Mr. Smythe. "What are they carrying on their heads?"

"It might be almost anything. Laundry, or fruit from the market, or loaves from the bakery." Before Liza could re-erupt into speech, he added quickly, "There are the offices. We use the upper two floors as a warehouse."

I looked at a pale green stucco building. Above its entrance a sign read, "Fonsell and Haverly, Inc." The sight of those two familiar names in this exotic place brought me a sense of incongruity, almost as if I had glimpsed our frock-coated minister moving through the sidewalk crowd of turbaned women, dark-skinned, barefooted men in white cotton shirts and trousers, and occasional Europeans, whose ordinary business dress contrasted oddly with the pith helmets shadowing their faces.

At the far side of the plaza, the carriage stopped before the hotel, a three-story white building with lacy iron balconies and tall jalousied doors. Paul Ronsard, leaving the carriage first, helped Ephraim to the ground, and then turned back to me. "Do you think you'll be settled by tomorrow afternoon? Perhaps we could go shell hunting."

"I'd like that very much."

The carriage moved past two more buildings, and then turned onto a dirt road leading away from the plaza. On either side, separated from the road by low stucco walls, and surrounded by a luxuriant tangle of palmettos and scarlet hibiscus, were houses of one or two stories. I asked Mr. Smythe, "Who lives in these houses?"

"Middle-class people. Native shopkeepers and a few English civil servants. The wealthier people, of course, live on plantations in the interior. Some are English, but others are descendants of French families who were here before Napoleon lost the island to the English."

An open carriage moved toward us. Its passenger, a blond, Junoesque woman clad in frilly white, bowed to Mr. Smythe. He tipped his pith helmet. "That was a member of one of our French families," he told me a moment later. "Her husband has a sugar plantation near the Atlantic side of the island."

"And where do you live?"

"On the other side of the plaza, on a street similar to this one."

Less than a minute later, the carriage stopped before the two-story house Mr. Smythe had rented for Liza and me. Against the trees which surrounded it—several varieties of palm, and some unfamiliar trees with large leaves as lustrous as northern holly—the white stucco house gave an impression of coolness. Before we were halfway up the walk, its flagstones blue-white in the late afternoon shadows, the jalousied front door opened. I saw a stately, coal-black woman of middle age, in a white turban and a white, full-skirted dress. I realized that she must be the housekeeper-cook. Standing a respectful pace to the rear was a somewhat younger mulatto woman, presumably the nursemaid.

Mr. Smythe made the introductions. The housekeeper's name was Abigail Harkness, and the nursemaid's Jeanne Bouvet. "Well," he said to me, "I trust you will be comfortable."

"I'm sure we will."

He shook my hand, and went down the walk. I said to the nursemaid, "Perhaps we had best get Liza settled first."

The mulatto woman nodded. "She and I have rooms upstairs." Then, to Liza: "Come, *ma petite*." My daughter, who had been looking at Jeanne with wide, appraising eyes, evidently liked what she saw, because she willingly took the woman's hand. On the second floor I inspected the pleasantly furnished room—wicker tables and chairs, a small brass bed, and a big china lamp, already lit—which had been assigned to Liza. Then I went downstairs. In the wide lower hall the housekeeper was lighting oil lamps that hung from wall brackets. I had entered this house in full daylight. Now, with tropical abruptness, it was night.

Abigail said, in her pleasant West Indian accent, "I have given you the downstairs bedroom. It opens onto the garden."

Following her down the hall, I entered a large, airy room. The glow from a china lamp with a crystal base showed me a four-poster bed, a rosewood dressing table, a polished floor that was bare except for a fluffy white rug beside the bed. The housekeeper said, "Did Mr. Smythe tell you that I go home after dinner each night? I have a husband, you see, and three children."

"No, he didn't tell me, but it's perfectly all right."

"I can serve dinner in an hour. Will that be too soon?"

"No, that will be fine."

An hour later in the high-ceilinged dining room, I ate fish with a lemon-flavored sauce, and a vegetable dish that combined okra and green peppers. The food was good, but as I sat there at the candlelighted table I realized that never before, except when I was confined to bed, had I eaten dinner all by myself.

Returning to my room, I opened the jalousied doors that led to the garden. An almost full moon was up now, sending a flood of radiance down from a sky that was nearer purple than blue. I moved along the graveled path. Just beyond a stone bench stood a small palm tree, with white flowers blooming from between the scales of its thick trunk. Orchids, I thought wonderingly, wild orchids growing right here in my temporary garden. As I reached out to touch a petal, a bird somewhere near by in the darkness uttered three low, sweet notes. The thought came to me, "A night made for love."

My hand fell away from the disturbingly flesh-like petal. Turning, I moved along the walk. I thought, "I'm close to twenty-three." Twenty-three, and alone. And unless that plumed knight appeared, or unless I divorced Jason soon and went out to look for him, I was apt to remain alone.

Suddenly the night's beauty seemed intolerable. I went into my room and closed the doors.

Paul Ronsard called the next afternoon. By then my mood of the night before had vanished, and I was able to meet him with smiling composure. We drove down to the beach that stretched on either side of the wharf and walked on the fine, pinkish sand. We found no pirate gold, but shells were everywhere—tiny bivalves of various shades, pink-lined conchs, several species of chambered nautilus, and a fluted, fragilely beautiful white whelk which Paul said was called a paper whelk. Although we were never out of sight of the *Kestrel* lying with the two schooners alongside the wharf, neither of us mentioned Jason.

During the week that followed, I saw Paul every day. We added to my shell collection. We walked around the plaza, looking at shopwindow displays of bread, of fish and shellfish, of native straw hats and baskets, and—surprisingly to me—of fine bone china from England, and kid gloves and perfume from France. On still another day we drove in a hired buggy a mile or so up a tortuous road that led up into the jungle-clad mountains. When the road became impassable, we got out and walked the rest of the way to a fort that dated from the island's Spanish days. Vines were interlaced over its crumbling stucco walls and over the rusty cannon pointing out across the turquoise and aquamarine waters of the bay.

Twice during that week I caught a glimpse of Jason, once crossing the plaza with Claude Smythe, and again as a distant but unmistakable figure on the *Kestrel*'s quarterdeck. Finally I asked Paul if Jason had been staying at the hotel. He had spent two nights there, Paul said, but the rest of the time he had slept aboard the *Kestrel*.

Late one morning I heard Abigail admitting a visitor to the house. Thinking that he was Paul, for some reason arriving before lunch rather than after, I stepped from my room into the hall. Jason stood just inside the front door, dressed in his dark blue uniform despite the tropic heat, and carrying his visored cap in his hand.

I moved toward him. He said, with a slight smile that did not reach his eyes, "I thought you might like to look over the sugar crop I've contracted for. That is, if you're not busy."

I tried to keep the constraint I felt out of my voice. "I'm not busy."

He had hired an open carriage and a driver for our tour. Once we had passed the last of the houses, the street became a road walled by jungle. Interlaced through the trees—many of the West Indian varieties of mahogany, Jason said—were vines thick as a man's waist. Brightly colored parrots and finches flashed through the dim light beyond the first line of trees, and once a reddish creature with a rabbitlike body and a squirrellike head scurried across the road, causing the horse to rear. It was an agouti, Jason said. Largely nocturnal animals, they appeared so seldom by day that horses were not accustomed to them.

A few minutes later the jungle walls gave way to fields of sugar cane, resembling vast stands of corn, but growing far taller than Long Island corn ever did. The canes often reached a height of fifteen feet, Jason told me. He went on to explain that with the favorable conditions prevailing in San Isidro—rich, volcanic soil and plentiful rainfall in October and November—cane grew so fast that growers could make several cuttings a year, stripping the cornlike leaves away before severing the jointed stalks. "These fields have been cut twice this year. D'Auberge will make at least one more cutting."

"I don't see any workers in the field."

"That's because it's between harvests. Now everyone's busy turning the cane into raw sugar." He sniffed the air. "They must be running the coppers right now. We'll find out for sure soon." I could smell the boiling sugar too, a cloying sweetness in the air.

The carriage turned off onto a narrow road running through the field. To my left, on high ground above the sea of cane, rose an impressive house of what appeared to be white limestone, its second floor balcony supported by pillars. "That's the d'Auberge house," he said. "They're in Haiti right now." He paused. "But they are giving a dinner party next Thursday night. We are invited. Would you care to go?"

I asked, obscurely angered by his offhand tone, "Would it be best? For appearance sake?"

"I suppose so."

"All right, then," I said, and started thinking about what I should wear. Fortunately, after considerable indecision, I had brought with me an evening dress of brown taffeta, and black jet earrings and a necklace and a black lace fan to go with it. The dress was several years out of date, but probably, in this out-of-the-way place, that wouldn't matter. Still, I reflected uneasily, some of the Frenchwomen I had glimpsed from time to time looked very smart.

Jason broke in on my thoughts. "That's the sugar house, up ahead." I saw a long, low wooden structure at one side of the road. "Probably you won't want to go any farther than the doorway."

He explained then that the sugar cane was chopped up

and its juice squeezed from it. After treatment with lime, to reduce its acidity, the juice was put into evaporating pans, to reduce its water content. After that the clarified and concentrated juice was boiled in huge copper kettles until the sugar crystallized, and a mass consisting of sugar crystal and molasses was formed. Then the mass was placed in perforated hogsheads, so that the molasses could drain off. "D'Auberge makes the molasses into rum," he said, "and I take the raw sugar to New Jersey."

Later on, I thought, he would take the sugar to his own refinery in Sag Harbor. In spite of all that had happened to me there, I felt, and not for the first time on this lush island, a longing for my native village. That contradictory village, with its Long Wharf built to reach out and gather in the world's riches, and its tall church steeple, built largely by those same riches, pointing sternly to a realm where the poor and the meek would have first right of entry.

The carriage stopped, and Jason and I walked to the wide doorway of the long shed. Almost immediately I retreated several paces. The sugar smell and the heat of the charcoal fires under the huge kettles were overwhelming. Jason said, with a slight smile, "I gather you don't want the rest of the conducted tour."

We returned to the carriage. "Take us back to town," Jason told the driver, and then said to me, "I'm meeting some men at the hotel for lunch. Besides, I imagine Ronsard will be calling for you."

"Yes." Until then I had not been sure that he knew of my daily excursions with Paul.

He said, as the carriage turned onto the road leading back to town, "I hope you don't find life too dull here."

"I don't." True, Abigail would not allow me to help with the housework. She had looked shocked and offended when I offered to. But I managed to fill up my days by seeing Paul, and reading the books he loaned me, and playing with Liza in her room or in the garden. I had also written long letters to Dr. Cantrell, and to the Presbyterian minister, and to Rose Murphy. My letter to Rose had been in reply to one I received from her only a few days after I reached San Isidro. The Biemeyers, she wrote, had offered her an increase in wages to stay with them. It seemed that their married son and his wife, who was expecting, had come to live with them. If I did not mind, now that Liza was no longer a baby . . .

I had written back, congratulating her on her new salary, and saying that I was sure I could manage Liza from now on.

The carriage, emerging from between the jungle walls, passed the first of the small houses. I said tentatively, "I haven't had a chance to really talk to you about this. You were so—busy before we left Sag Harbor, and on the ship too. But anyway, I'm sorry that I went to see your mother without consulting you first."

He said, not looking at me, "That's all right. I was angry then but—well, I can see how Annabelle led you into it."

After an interval I asked, "Does she have any explanation of why she came to see me that day?"

"I don't know. I haven't seen her for the last six months."

Six months. Then he had broken with her many weeks before she appeared at the Howard Street house. No wonder she had wanted to stir up trouble. Well, she had certainly succeeded. That shouting match between Jason and me in the Fonsell garden. And then that stormy evening two days later, as I started down to the second floor of the house on Howard Street . . .

He said, as if his thoughts had followed mine, "Does that wound on your head still give you any trouble?"

"None at all."

Despite the blood on that poker, my wound had been only superficial. As for the poker itself, Jerry Duane, our local constable, determined the next day that it had come

165

from a set of fireplace tools in one of the second floor bedrooms. He was also able to tell me, as he sat beside my bed in the Fonsell house, how my assailant had made his exit. A kitchen window had been left wide open. Unfortunately, the rain which had left a pool of water on the kitchen floor had also erased any footprints on the ground below the window.

"I think, ma'am, that it was a tramp. He slept in the house the night before, probably on the parlor sofa you mentioned. If he was drunk, he'd have stretched out on the first soft spot he found."

"But why didn't he leave in the morning?"

"Because he looked around after he woke up, and saw that there were things he could carry away, if he waited until dark."

"Are you sure he was in the house when I arrived? Couldn't he have come in later? I left the back door open. I mean, if he had been there since the night before, wouldn't he have cooked some food? Even if he'd brought no food with him, there were jars of green beans and vegetable soup in the cellar. He could have warmed some of that up."

"And sent smoke out of the stovepipe, for the neighbors to see?" His plump face, wreathed in muttonchop whiskers, exuded tolerant superiority.

I said, "I didn't think of that."

"Well, anyway, ma'am, I think he was in the house when you drove up. He dashed up to the second floor and hid in a bedroom, hoping you'd leave after a while. Then, moving around in the dark, he knocked over a fire screen. I found it lying on the floor in the bedroom the poker came from. He knew you must have heard him, and that you'd run to the neighbors and give the alarm. Could be, you know, that he was wanted for something pretty bad somewhere else, and couldn't risk your getting him arrested. So he picked up the poker, and waited for you in the bedroom doorway."

I had accepted his explanation, chiefly because I wanted to. It was infinitely preferable to think of my assailant as a thieving tramp, rather than as someone who knew me, someone who had come to that house for the express purpose of attacking me.

But even though I had accepted Constable Duane's theory, I still shrank from the thought of Liza and me being left in a manless household when the *Kestrel* sailed. And so, as soon as I was able to, I had begun to prepare for the voyage.

The carriage had stopped before the tree-shadowed white stucco house, cool-looking even under the tropic noonday sun. Jason accompanied me up the walk. At the door he said, "I'm not sure what time the d'Auberges have set for Thursday night. I'll let you know."

"Thank you. And thank you for the tour."

"No need to thank me. After all, you have an interest in Fonsell and Haverly."

The next day, Wednesday, Paul Ronsard and I again went up to the old Spanish fort. Among the vegetation which covered the crumbling walls he had noticed some plants he had not seen elsewhere on the island. Probably, he said, some bored soldier a hundred years ago or more had whiled away his time by planting seeds or cuttings from other islands, or even from French or Spanish possessions in Africa. Anyway, he wanted to add the leaves to a collection he had begun to make. After he had picked the leaves and placed them inside the pages of a blank notebook, we sat on a rock outside the fort, and looked out over the water, and talked of that other island far to the north, the one we both called home.

The afternoon slipped away. The brief tropic dusk had begun to descend by the time we moved up the walk of the white stucco house. I said, "Do you know there are wild orchids in the garden here?"

"No, you never mentioned it."

167

"They're especially effective at this time of day. Would you like to see them?"

We moved down the wide, dim hall to where jalousied doors stood open. In the rapidly fading light, the delicate white orchids growing from the palm's trunk seemed to shimmer. We admired them for a moment and then began to move slowly along the garden path.

He asked, "Are you going to the d'Auberges' party tomorrow?"

"Yes, with Jason. Will you be there?"

"Yes." He paused, and then asked abruptly, "Do you plan to divorce Jason?"

Even though I had long been aware that Ephraim must have told his doctor of the circumstances of my marriage to Jason, the bluntness of the question surprised me. I said slowly, "I suppose so. For Liza's sake, though, I want to wait a while longer."

"I think I understand. You want the old talk to die down before you give people something new to talk about."

"Yes."

"And after the divorce?"

"I don't know. Who can see that far ahead?"

"Of late I've been thinking what a pity it is that I'm twenty-odd years older than you. If I were only ten years older, say, there might be a place for me in your plans."

I said, touched and disconcerted, "Oh, Paul."

He stopped, tipped my chin with a bent forefinger, and kissed me lightly. "Don't look so upset. It's not your fault I had the bad judgment to be born at the wrong time."

As we moved on down the walk, he added, "Besides, maybe later on you'll decide you can forgive my bad timing. Lately I've thought of going out west, perhaps to Denver, in a year or two. There are already three doctors in Southampton, and a young man still in medical school plans to practice there. That will be too many doctors for a town that size.

Perhaps by the time I'm ready to leave, you'll be willing to marry me and come with me."

We had reached the end of the path. Turning, we started back toward the house. "Anyway," he said, "keep it in mind."

"I will."

And I would. I did not love Paul, but I liked and respected him very much. As for the difference in age, it seemed to me that didn't matter greatly. He not only looked younger than his years, he was youthful in his varied interests.

"Denver's a growing city," he said, "and a beautiful one. I took a vacation out there four—"

He broke off. Following the direction of his gaze, I saw someone standing in the doorway, his figure a deeper dark against the dark hall. A moment later I realized it was Jason. How long, I wondered, had he been standing there? Long enough to have witnessed that kiss?

I said, in a constrained voice, "Why, hello, Jason."

"Hello." He nodded to Paul, and then turned back to me. "I came to tell you that I'll call for you at seven tomorrow night. The housekeeper said you were in the garden, so I just walked back here."

Light bloomed in the hallway behind him. I could see Abigail, holding a lighted taper to the wick of still another wall lamp. I could also make out the expression—or rather lack of it—on Jason's face. I thought, feeling an odd mixture of dismay and gratification, "He's angry."

"I'll be here at seven," he repeated. "Well, good night." Turning, he strode down the hall.

When the front door had closed behind Jason, Paul looked down at me. He said, in a tone of wry discovery, "Now you *are* upset."

"It was embarrassing, that was all."

"Was it?" he asked lightly. "Well, I'll see you at the d'Auberges'. No, don't bother to show me out."

Chapter 19

AS SOON AS I heard Jason's voice in the hall the next night, I left my room. I moved toward him, an embroidered shawl around shoulders left bare by the brown taffeta dress, and my black lace fan dangling from my wrist. He watched me approach, his face as dark—and as impassive—as an Indian's above his ruffled white evening shirt.

I said, "Hello, Jason," and then added nervously, "I hope the other ladies are not too fine. This dress is five years old."

Perhaps, in a phrase used by the girls at the Misses Pride's school, I was fishing for a compliment. If so, I did not catch one. "I'm sure your dress is quite suitable," he said, not looking at it, and conducted me out to the hired carriage we had used two days before.

When the street became the jungle-walled road, he said, "The *Josiah Purcell* is sailing early tomorrow morning." The *Purcell*, tied up near the *Kestrel*, was a trading schooner out of Boston.

"Oh?"

"I must see the schooner's captain on business tonight. I'll have to leave the d'Auberges' early. Ronsard will see you home."

"Oh," I said again, but in a different tone. The rest of the way we made stiff conversation about the *Purcell*'s cargo—West Indian mahogany—and about the *Kestrel*'s sailing, scheduled for a week from the next day. I had an almost irresistible urge to say, "You were angry last night. Why were you?" But I couldn't ask that, not unless he himself brought up the subject. The carriage left us at the foot of the d'Auberges' front steps, and we climbed toward the sounds of talk and laughter spilling through the wide doorway.

For a few minutes after we entered the high-ceilinged reception hall, my mind was empty of everything except dismay over my attire. Madame d'Auberge, in intricately tucked and flounced pale blue satin, stood beside her thin, wiry husband under a huge crystal chandelier. A diamond tiara glittered on her sleek dark hair. More diamonds encircled her throat. Other women moving through a wide doorway into what must be a drawing room looked almost as magnificent. But at least in that first appalled look around me, I saw a few women, unmistakably English, whose serene dowdiness was a comfort.

Madame d'Auberge greeted us graciously and then indicated, with a flick of her ivory fan toward the archway, that apéritifs were being served in the drawing room. When we joined the chattering crowd beyond the archway, Jason took two fragile glasses from a tray held by a footman in knee breeches, and handed one to me. As I sipped the apéritif, Jason told me, in stiffly polite tones, what little he knew of the other guests. With the exception of a few English civil servants and businessmen and their wives, they were all French planters of San Isidro and the neighboring islands. At last, after Jason had consumed a second apéritif, one of the footmen opened a pair of ceiling-high doors, ornamented with gold scrollwork, and announced dinner.

I found my place card between that of Mr. Claude Smythe and a Monsieur Étienne Duvall. Mr. Smythe greeted me pleasantly and then pointed out his wife, a plump little woman, seated halfway down the long table, who had somehow managed to keep her lovely English complexion despite the tropic sun. As for the Frenchman, perhaps he sensed my dismay over the brown taffeta, for he lost little time in telling me that he found my appearance ravishing. "And the dress, Madame, the dress! Such a wise choice. For the youthful beauty, simplicity is always the best choice. The flounces, the jewelry, bah! They only distract from what really interests *les hommes*."

The food was as rich as Monsieur Duvall's compliments. A lobster bisque, then fish with a creole sauce, and then pheasant—brought over from Port-au-Prince, Mr. Smythe told me. After that, roast lamb served with a mint sauce and vegetables. Finally, a meringue decorated with candied violets.

The trouble was that each course was accompanied by its own wine. I tried to keep up with the others for a while, and then, my head spinning, turned down the remaining glasses aligned before my plate. But Jason, I noticed, was emptying his wineglasses about as rapidly as a footman could fill them. He sat near the other end of the table, between a middle-aged Englishwoman and the handsome blond French-woman to whom Mr. Smythe had tipped his pith helmet the day of my arrival in San Isidro. Whenever he was not talking to one or the other of his dinner partners, his face held a set, remote expression. If he looked in my direction, I did not see him do so.

The dessert plates had been removed. Now, at long last, Madame d'Auberge would rise, signaling that the ladies were to retire for the coffee I very much needed, while the men remained at table to smoke cigars and drink brandy. But she did not. Evidently San Isidro islanders did not do things that way, at least not the French islanders. Coffee plus brandy and other liqueurs were served to all of us. On Mr. Smythe's advice, I allowed a footman to fill my glass with a green liquid. "It's mint-flavored. Very refreshing after dinner."

It was mint-flavored, all right. It was also potent.

At last Madame d'Auberge rose. But the evening was not over. We moved back into the drawing room, where gilt chairs had been set up in rows facing an ivory-colored grand piano. Paul, appearing at my side, led me to seats on the aisle. "Jason has business to attend to," he said. "I'm to take you home."

"I know." If Jason tried to transact business tonight, I reflected grimly, he would probably get the worst of it. He had drunk far more wine than I had, plus two glasses of brandy, and he probably was little more used to such indulgence than I was. At least I had never seen him drink more than one glass of wine at any meal in the Fonsell house.

I sat there, tipsy and miserable, while a plump contralto in green velvet sang French songs I couldn't understand.

Eventually, though, I was driving through the soft dark night beside Paul. I said, "I had too much wine."

"I prescribe a good night's sleep. As for what else ails you, I'm afraid I don't have a prescription."

I said, untruthfully and a bit snappishly, "I don't know what you mean."

He smiled. "Then let's forget I said it."

When he left me at my door he said, "I may receive word from that hospital on the other side of the island tomorrow. I wrote asking when I could visit their wards. But if I don't go there, would you like to go for a drive?"

"Yes, very much. Good night, Paul."

I moved down the hallway to my room. I was in my nightgown, and about to blow out the light, when I heard the front door open. Footsteps came striding down the hall. Hastily I reached for my dressing gown and struggled into it.

The door of my room opened. Jason stood there, still in evening clothes, his face dark and angry above the white shirt front. He moved toward me, seized my shoulders, and gave them a little shake. "Go ahead," he invited. "Go ahead and scream."

I looked up at him, with the pulse pounding so hard in the hollow of my throat that I was sure he could see it.

"Now you listen to me," he said, and gave me another

shake. "Steven was right about the way I felt. I've felt that way ever since you were about seventeen years old. But first Steven was in the way, and now this damned Ronsard. Well, we'll see about that, we'll just see."

He pulled me against him and kissed me, hard. I felt the shock of that kiss clear down to the soles of my feet. For a second or so I was too limp to move. Then I wound my arms around his neck. Dimly I was aware that my mouth had grown soft and accepting beneath his. Bending, he lifted me in his arms and carried me to the bed.

When I awoke the next morning, I lay with closed eyes for a few seconds, wondering why I was so happy. Then I remembered. Opening my eyes, I turned onto one elbow. Jason no longer lay beside me, although the pillow still bore the impress of his head.

Well, probably he was having breakfast. As swiftly as I could, I rose, washed my face, dressed. When I went out into the hallway, I saw Abigail moving toward me, a white envelope in her hand. She said, "When I came here this morning, I found this under the front door."

I took the envelope, thanked her, and went back to my room. With unsteady fingers I opened the envelope and unfolded the single sheet of paper inside. My gaze went to the signature. Jason's. Then I read the note.

"By the time you read this," he had written in a small, neat hand, "I will have sailed as a passenger on the *Purcell*. I have instructed my chief officer to supervise the loading of the *Kestrel*, and to act as captain when she sails a week from now. He will choose another chief mate from the several qualified men who have made application to Mr. Smythe at our offices here. You and Liza, together with my father and Dr. Ronsard, can return home on the *Kestrel*."

The handwriting changed, became ragged and larger. "You'll never know how sorry I am about last night. You'd had too much wine. There's a word for a man who takes advantage of such a situation, and the word isn't gentleman. I was fairly drunk, but not enough so that I can find an excuse for myself.

"As soon as you get to Sag Harbor, we will discuss divorce, and other living arrangements pending divorce. I will agree to anything you ask. —Jason."

I reread the last two paragraphs. "Oh, Jason," I said aloud, "you utter fool," and realized that I was laughing even though there were tears on my face.

It would be a week until the *Kestrel* sailed. It would take two weeks to reach home, even less if we made no stop except the New Jersey port. And so in about three weeks I would be able to tell Jason in person what a fool he was.

I was at breakfast when Paul Ronsard arrived. He said, walking into the dining room, "No, don't get up. Finish your breakfast. I just came to say that we'll have to postpone our drive. I'm going over to the hospital today."

"Oh, that's all right," I said gaily. "Wouldn't you like something? Eggs? Coffee?"

"No, thanks. I've had breakfast." He studied me. "Do you know that Jason has sailed on the *Purcell*? His chief mate will act as captain on our return voyage."

"Yes, I know."

"When did Jason tell you? Last night?"

"No, not then," I said, and felt the warm blood rush into my face. "I mean, I didn't know until this morning."

"I see." He smiled, but his gray eyes look wry. "As I told you, my timing is very bad. If I had spoken a year ago, or even a few months ago— Well," he finished briskly, "I'd better start. It's a long drive to the other side of the island."

Less than three weeks later, on a clear, moonless night, the *Kestrel* slipped into her berth beside Long Wharf. I was in the cabin I had shared with Liza when I heard Jason's voice on deck. "Wait here, darling," I said to my daughter

175

who, cloaked and bonneted, sat on the lower berth kicking her heels against its framework. "I'll be back in a minute."

I hurried to the companionway and climbed onto the deck. Jason and the *Kestrel*'s acting captain were descending the ladder from the quarterdeck. I called, "Jason."

He said something to the other man and then walked slowly toward me. "Hello, Irene." His voice sounded carefully controlled. "Did you have a pleasant voyage?"

"Not in the least. I was too impatient to get back here so that I could tell you something."

After a moment he asked, "What is it you have to say?"

My voice and my smile shook. "That you're a fool, an utter, utter fool."

He understood. He didn't reach out to touch me, nor even speak for several seconds. But his very stillness told me that he had understood.

At last he said, in an oddly roughened voice, "Go on home with the others. I have to stay here for a little while. But I'll come to your room in about an hour, and then we can talk about what a fool I am."

Chapter 20

WE WERE HAPPY, Jason and I, that fall and winter.

Early in October and again in January, the *Kestrel* made voyages to San Isidro, but Jason stayed at home. He felt that his former chief mate, now captain, could handle transactions with Claude Smythe and d'Auberge. Besides, the refinery needed his attention. Because of bad weather and delayed deliveries of materials, work on the foundation had proceeded slowly. In November and December, too, construction had been hampered by sleet and snow. Thus it was not until late January that the still-unfinished building was ready for the installation of its machinery.

One clear, very cold afternoon the last week of January, Jason took me to see the machinery. While carpenters hammered on the exterior walls and the roof, he pointed out the conveyor belt which, powered by a steam engine, would carry raw sugar to huge vats filled with water. Bone black—"that's charcoal made from animal bones"—would be added to the mixture to remove impurities. Then, by means of machinery yet to be installed, the sugar would be recrystallized into a fine white powder.

"Technically," he said, "the final product will be invert sugar."

"It will be what?"

"Invert sugar. You see, sweetheart, if you take a plane of polarized light—" He explained the rest of it, something about how raw sugar rotates light to the right, and refined sugar to the left.

I said, uncomprehending but impressed, "Think of that! Well, no matter what it's called, let's hope people like the taste."

After we left the refinery we drove south on Main Street. The bright sun, touching ice-encased twigs of trees, turned them into prisms, so that again and again I saw a brief flash of rainbow colors. People in other vehicles greeted us, the women bowing slightly, the men raising their hats. None of them looked at Jason with the scorn I had seen in old Mr. Hiram's face. But it seemed to me that their eyes held a wary reserve, as if—in spite of the *Kestrel*'s successful voyages, in spite of the nearly completed refinery—they were waiting to make a final judgment.

I thought, "Perhaps if we gave a few parties . . ."

There had been Christmas festivity at the Fonsell house, but except for the presence of Paul Ronsard and John R. Solum, it had been a family party. I had invited John Solum one day when, as I drove over the bridge toward Main Street, I had seen him trudging along in the opposite direction. To my surprise, he had actually appeared on Christmas Eve, wearing outmoded but once expensive evening clothes. He had looked briefly at his portraits of Julia Fonsell and of Liza, and pronounced them "pretty good." After that he had sat almost totally silent, glass in hand, for two hours. Then, late in the evening, he had launched suddenly into a dissertation on some new French painters whom none of us except Paul had ever heard of. These men—impressionists, he called them—were "painting sunlight by breaking up color," whatever that meant. And French composers were doing new and wonderful things too, using "unprepared for and unresolved dissonances." Again I felt that Paul was the only one who had the vaguest notion of what he was talking about.

John Solum said, "I think I'll go back to Paris." As if he intended to start across the Atlantic within the next ten minutes, he got to his feet, shook hands all around, and left the house.

Yes, it had been a good Christmas, the happiest of my life. And for me it would have been even happier if that round-faced woman in Green Corners had been present. With Jason's consent I had taken Liza to Green Corners in late November, and had asked his mother to spend Christmas with us. "No, Irene," she said firmly, "Jason wouldn't really like that, no matter what he says. He'd be afraid I might meet some folks who'd hurt my feelings. Maybe someday . . ."

Someday, when and if Jason became so important that no one would dare to "hurt the feelings" of the woman who had borne him.

I said, "Jason, would it be all right if we gave a small party, say six or seven couples?"

"Soon, you mean?"

"Fairly soon. Before we know it, Liza will be going to school. Wouldn't it be better if we were—well, on closer terms with parents of the other children?"

He was silent for several seconds, his gaze apparently directed between the mare's pointed ears to the small cloud of steam rising from her nostrils. Then he said, "Would you mind waiting until after the refinery is opened? I don't think Liza will have any trouble after that. The refinery will be good for this town. Oh, I don't suppose Fonsell and Haverly will ever employ as many men as the whaling fleet did. Around two thousand men used to make a living out of that. But still—"

I waited. After a moment he went on, with seeming irrelevance, "I don't remember California at all. About my earliest clear memory is of my father, one day down at the cove. He told me that at one time Sag Harbor handled even more cargo than New York. 'It's never been a big town,' he said, 'but its ships made it famous all over the world. Why, people in Australia, say, who never heard of St. Louis knew about

Sag Harbor.' He was always talking about the town, and the great whaling days, and the War of 1812, and the Revolution, and how Fonsells had been part of all of it. By the time I was old enough to go to school, I figured that being a Fonsell of Sag Harbor made me about the luckiest boy in the world."

After a moment he went on, "School! Do you have any idea what small boys can do to you once they get hold of the word bastard? Until I was twelve, I don't think a week passed without my giving someone a bloody nose, or getting one. But it didn't make me want to leave, not even when I got old enough to leave. I was still a Fonsell, and this was still my town."

At long last, I understood my husband. It was not ambition for riches, or for power, which drove him. Put quite simply, he loved his town, warts and all, and he wanted it to love him back.

I turned my head, so that he would not know that tears had sprung to my eyes. And then, mistily, I saw a snowy lawn, a pillared porch, a fanlighted door. I thought, with a shaky smile, "I hope his town doesn't get so rich that it tears down these houses."

I turned back to him. "All right, darling. The party can wait. I'd like to have the inside of the house painted first, anyway, starting with the third floor. It's awfully shabby."

"All right. Go ahead." He paused, and then asked, "You still don't like that house, do you?"

"I've liked living there these past few months."

"So have I, sweetheart, so have I. But that hasn't changed anything that's happened there, has it?"

No, it hadn't. Even these days I sometimes would think of my aunt's crumpled body in the lower hall, or of Julia Fonsell's faceless, nameless destroyer, wielding his club that long-ago moonlit night.

Jason said, "I've never liked it either, and not just because of things that happened in it." He paused, and then burst out, "It's so damned ugly."

I looked at him in surprise. Always I had thought that he, like his father, admired those stucco-coated pillars, and that gray-green skylight swelling up inside the railed widow's walk.

"My father designed it himself, you know, while he was on a voyage." Jason chuckled. "I've always figured he was drunk at the time."

I said happily, "Then you'd rather live somewhere else?"

"Yes, and we will, after my father's gone. We couldn't move him now, at his age. But later on—well, Ruth can live there."

Yes, Ruth would never leave. I said, "Is that why you haven't suggested selling the Howard Street house?" I had wondered about that. The machinery had cost more than he had expected, far more, in fact, than the refinery building itself. And yet he had never broached the subject of our selling my aunt's house.

"Yes, that's why. I thought you might like to live there again, someday." He grinned at me. "We can put a plaque up in the parlor, where I proposed to you."

I laughed, and pressed my cheek against his shoulder. "We'd better get home. Liza will be waking from her nap soon."

At Glover Street we turned, crossed the railroad tracks, and then moved along Water Street, skirting the cove. Children skated over the blue-gray ice, tassels of their red and green and brown stocking caps bobbing, voices clear and sweet on the cold air. On the North Haven shore, beech trees made their precise, spade-shaped patterns against the pale blue sky. "I like winter," I thought. "It's so simple and clean, so peaceful."

Those were the last few peaceful moments we were to have that day. When we emerged from the private road into the clearing, we saw Dr. Cantrell's buggy drawn up at the steps. And despite the closed windows, we could hear Ephraim inside, bellowing with pain and rage.

We found Ruth in the lower hall, hovering near the den's open doorway. "He slipped on the garden walk," she said. "His leg's broken."

"Better wait here," Jason said to me, and went into the den.

She and Mrs. Burlow, Ruth told me, had managed to get Ephraim inside and onto the couch in his den. Then Ruth had gone for Dr. Cantrell. I could tell she was distressed, and yet even now that little smile curved her lips. I said, "Where is Mrs. Burlow?"

"In the kitchen. She's awfully angry."

I didn't bother to ask why. I hurried upstairs, found Liza still asleep, and hurried down again. Ruth still hovered beside the den's partly opened door. Ephraim was roaring at Jason now. "Son, get this butcher out of here. He's killing me."

Dr. Cantrell answered, "I doubt that anything could kill you. And you can't expect me to set your leg without hurting you."

"Jason, get me my own doctor!"

"Shut up," Dr. Cantrell said. "I'll be only too happy to turn you over to Dr. Ronsard. But right now, I'm the only doctor you've got."

"I won't swallow that stuff!"

"Jason, get behind him. Hold his nose, if you have to." A few seconds later he said, through Ephraim's enraged, spluttering bellow, "You'll feel better now. And quieter."

Followed by Jason, Dr. Cantrell emerged into the hall, his black bag in his hand. "He'll sleep for a while. It will be up to Dr. Ronsard, of course, but I feel he shouldn't be moved to his bedroom. It would only cause more pain. And that couch is wide enough." He shook his head wonderingly. "Almost anyone else that age would have broken a hip. He only breaks a leg. Well, I'll be getting along. Goodbye Ruth, Irene. Goodbye, Jason."

"Goodbye," Ruth said, and turned to climb the stairs.

Jason and I walked with Dr. Cantrell to the door. When it had closed behind him, I turned to see Mrs. Burlow hurrying toward us. Her sharp nose seemed to quiver with rage. "Mrs. Fonsell, I'm giving two weeks' notice."

"You can't!" I cried. "Not now, when my father-in-law—"

"He's the reason." She turned to my husband. "The things he said when we were bringing him into the house! If I told you, you wouldn't believe me."

"Try me," Jason said.

She ignored that. "I didn't know there were such words."

"Then there was no harm done. If you didn't know the words, you didn't know what they meant."

"Jason!" I cried warningly.

"Mr. Fonsell, I'm a decent woman, and I won't stay here. Anyway, I've got another offer. Mrs. Spiering, over in Bridgehampton. So I'm giving my two weeks' notice."

"We don't want your notice," Jason said. "You can pack it with the rest of your things. If you're ready in ten minutes, I'll drop you at the depot on my way to get Dr. Ronsard."

Chin elevated, she climbed the stairs. "Oh, Jason," I said, "how could you? With your father needing care, there'll be more work—"

"Couldn't you get Rose Murphy?"

"Not when the Biemeyers need her so much. Besides, she's all wrapped up in that grandson of theirs."

"Well, don't worry. We'll get Carl Johansen's wife."

"Your foreman's?"

"Yes. She works out by the day. And she's a nice woman. You'll like her."

Chapter 21

I DID LIKE Mrs. Johansen. A recent immigrant from Sweden, she was as blond and almost as tall as her husband, and seemed almost tireless. Arriving at eight each morning, she would work beside me—cleaning, cooking, dishwashing—until, at five o'clock, Jason drove her home to the Johansen house on Division Street. Furthermore, she was the sort of woman who enjoys challenges. Ephraim's ill temper was a challenge. By cheerfully ignoring his most profane outbursts, she soon reduced him to a state resembling meekness. The three painters, when they arrived the second week in February, were another challenge. Far from complaining about the clutter on the third floor, she stepped briskly over buckets and around ladders, and talked in Swedish with the boss painter, a Mr. Sanstrom of Easthampton who, she told me, was a second cousin of hers.

Once she even solved a minor crisis. Mr. Sanstrom found that the gears and lever, designed to raise the domed skylight from the circular wooden base upon which it rested, were frozen with rust. So how, he inquired, could they calk and paint all surfaces of the base, the way Mrs. Fonsell wanted?

"You're big, strong fallers," Mrs. Johansen said. "Yoost yimmy it open."

Standing on ladders, they did jimmy it open, with crowbars. Two of the men, heaving and sweating, pushed the dome back until only its hinged portion touched the base. Then their companion propped the skylight open with a stout two-by-six.

That same afternoon, a raw, cloudy one, Jason took me over the bridge to see the rest of the machinery, installed only the day before. I listened admiringly but without much comprehension as he described the workings of all those belts and wheels and cogs and boilers.

When we returned to the house I went into the den and found my father-in-law restless and coughing and flushed of face. I measured out the mild sedative Paul Ronsard had prescribed, helped him sit halfway up to drink it, and then went into the dining room. Jason stood at the long table, studying outspread diagrams of the newly installed machinery. He looked up. "How is he?"

"Not good. Feverish. And his cough is worse."

Jason frowned. "Paul's coming this afternoon. Maybe he'll spend the night here, if Dad's really in a bad way."

After he had examined Ephraim, Paul himself suggested that we give him a room for the night. "I'm afraid of pneumonia," he said. "In the morning I'll decide whether or not he should be hospitalized."

Despite the worry he shared with us, Paul was, as always, a pleasant dinner companion. After dinner we sat for a while beside the dining room fireplace, talking of the *Kestrel*, soon to sail for home, and of San Isidro. Just once, as his gaze met mine, I felt that Paul was remembering the brief tropic dusk of a San Isidro garden. Then he went on talking of that island hospital. "It's surprisingly modern, even by American big-city standards. In fact, I found it cleaner than the Brooklyn hospital where I was in residence for a few months right after the War. The chief of staff and most of the doctors are British, but all the nurses are native." As he went on talking, his gray eyes turning from Jason to me and then back again, nothing in his manner suggested that he had ever stopped there on the graveled walk to kiss me, or ever asked me to marry him.

At ten, Jason showed him to the second floor room Mrs.

Johansen and I had prepared that afternoon. Then Jason and I went to the room that had once been his, but was now ours.

Sometime in the night I came abruptly awake. I sat bolt upright, my heart jumping. The room was filled with a reddish, flickering light that could mean only one thing. But I heard no ominous crackle, smelled no smoke. Then, through that flickering light, I saw Jason across the room, pulling suspender straps over his shoulders, and reaching inside the wardrobe for his coat.

"Jason! What is it?"

"There's fire in the village." Even as he spoke, I became aware of bells, wildly pealing the alarm.

I swung out of bed and crossed to the window. Shivering in the chill, I looked out over the cove to where pulsing, smoke-shrouded flames cast a reflection on lowering clouds. As nearly as I could judge, the fire was near the landward end of Long Wharf.

Fear tightened my stomach. Even though it had happened years before I was born, I had been raised on stories of the Great Fire of 1845, which had destroyed most of the lower part of the town. It had broken out that November night in a frame storehouse at the foot of Main Street. A strong westerly wind had driven the flames east and south through the village. Men and women and children, unable to penetrate the fire-walled canyon that lower Main Street had become, removed through the rear entrances of houses and shops and warehouses what few possessions they could carry in their arms. The firemen—then as now volunteers—had fought the flames with hand-pumped engines, in heat so intense that those of them still living carried burn scars of their battle.

The wind was westerly tonight. That fire over there— spreading now, its sullen light staining a larger area of low, scudding clouds—was near the spot where the 1845 fire had started. Turning, I asked, "Are you going to drive?"

"No, walk. If that fire is out of hand, it'll be bad enough

over there without adding another panicky horse to it." He opened the door. "Go back to bed. It's cold in here," he said, and closed the door behind him.

I did not go back to bed. Shivering, I turned around and looked through the window. There were flames farther south now, along Main Street. And it appeared to me that they were moving east, too. Swiftly, I began to dress.

A few minutes later, wearing a hooded cloak over a woolen dress, I knocked on Paul's door. "I'm awake," he answered immediately. "I'm getting dressed."

About a minute later he opened the door. "Why are you wearing a cloak? We won't have to leave. The fire can't possibly leap the cove."

"But I think it's starting along Bay Street. I've got to go over there. Will you go to Liza if she wakes up and starts crying?"

"Irene, you shouldn't go. What good can you do?"

"Jason's over there. I can be with him. Oh, Paul! If that refinery goes— He's worked so hard, hoped so hard."

Paul reached out and touched my cheek. "You love him a great deal, don't you?"

Unable to speak, I nodded.

"All right, then. I'll leave my door open, so that if Liza cries I'll hear her."

When I reached the road I saw that other North Haven residents were hurrying on foot toward the bridge. There was Mr. Seely, who owned a clothing store on Main Street, and old Mrs. Malvern, a shawl over her head, whose son was night clerk at the Nassau House, and Mr. Childers, an officer of the Suffolk County Bank. No one spoke to anyone else. We just hurried across the bridge, each person keeping close to the rail lest his foot slip on the ice-coated planks. Except for our short, hurrying footsteps, and the clamor of the bells, there was no sound.

On the opposite side of the cove, I moved with the others

across the railroad tracks and along the curving street that led to Long Wharf and the foot of Main Street. I could see now that structures built out along both sides of the wharf were ablaze. Near the wharf's bayward end, the masts and yards of a ship, outlined in flame, looked like some gigantic piece of fireworks.

At the foot of Main Street a fire engine pumped water from the public well, and volunteer firemen, their faces grim and frightened in the ruddy light, directed hoses at blazing Long Wharf, and at flames shooting up from one corner of the Nassau House on Main Street. Ignoring a fireman who yelled at me to go back, I skirted the fire apparatus and, aware of the heat from the burning hotel and the tavern next to it, started up Bay Street. The first two buildings along it had already caught fire. I brushed a blazing fragment of wood from my cloak, retreated to the bayward side of the street, and ran on. Dimly I was aware of dancing, rosy light at my left—the water's reflection of the burning village.

Two more buildings, as yet unharmed, over there on the right side of the street, and then the refinery. I stopped short, feeling a stunned incredulity. Why, they were tearing the refinery down! I could see them over there—two men wielding crowbars, and Jason swinging an ax. I heard a rasp of nails as a plank parted from its studding, and saw a flash of the fire's reflection on the ax blade as it bit into wood.

I started across the street. At the same moment Carl Johansen's tall figure emerged from the refinery doorway. "Mr. Fonsell! There's still time. I can get horses. We can haul your machinery out of there."

Not answering, Jason swung the ax. I stopped a few feet behind him, feeling a dismayed bewilderment.

"Mr. Fonsell! Are you crazy? If you'll let me get horses—"

"Carl, the fire's coming this way." Again he swung the ax. "If we raze this building and toss the wood into the bay, maybe we can stop it."

"Mr. Fonsell, save your machinery! It ain't insured, Mr. Fonsell. Save it!"

Jason shouted, "Get out of here. Go get grappling hooks, more axes, more men. You want the whole town to burn?"

No insurance. Jason had considered insurance. But it was expensive, and he had wanted to use every cent toward opening the refinery as soon as possible. I felt tears running down my face.

I said, "Jason."

He whirled around. "Irene! For God sake! Go home."

"Oh, Jason. I'm so—"

"You can't help me. Go home, darling. Go home, damn it."

I went. As I stumbled along, dazzled by the flames and by my tears, I could hear the rasp of nails and the shattering impact of the ax.

Nearing Long Wharf, I saw that a building on this side of it, the Maidstone Flour Mill, had caught fire. The heat at the foot of Main Street was even more intense now. Vaguely, I was aware of a crowd of men and women and children, gathered about a hundred yards up the street to watch the combat between the roaring flames and the pitifully inadequate fire engine. Dr. Cantrell stood much closer. Medical bag in hand, his plump face composed but alert, he stood on the west side of Main Street, with the flames reflected in his steel-rimmed spectacles. I circled around the firemen, holding my breath against the heated air, and headed along the street that curved toward the bridge.

From the corner of my eye I saw that the Huntting Building—that fine brick and stone structure that was supposed to be fireproof—now shot flames from beneath its overhanging roof. I thought of the night almost exactly four years before when I had danced with Jason at the Grand Ball there, and been acutely aware, without realizing the significance of my awareness, of his hand clasping my waist.

The bridge was just ahead. At its foot a woman stood motionless. As I drew closer I saw that it was Ruth. Her face, framed in a fur-lined hood, looked very pale. Her eyes, like Dr. Cantrell's glasses, reflected the flames.

"Ruth! Don't stay here. It's cold." A few snowflakes were drifting down now, not enough to help quench the fire, only enough to add to the misery of those who fought it.

She said, "I want to stay here."

"But why?"

"I just want to. I'll come home when they've put it out."

I had an eerie impression that she was standing guard, lest the conflagration somehow cross the bridge and threaten the ugly house that seemed to be the center, and only love, of her strange life. Or did she fear, I wondered fleetingly, not just the destruction of the house, but disclosure of some secret that lay within it?

I brushed the thought aside. "All right," I said, and turned away. I could not force her to come home. She was a grown woman, two years older than myself. I hurried on.

Halfway across the bridge I heard following footsteps. A man appeared at my side. "Did you know that no one has ever painted a blazing building? Oh, people have tried. But the results are always terrible, like cheap chromos."

I'd been grateful to John Solum for Liza's portrait. As for his rudeness, it had amused rather than annoyed me. But now I realized what a monster he was. For the second time in a generation, our village was threatened with destruction. This time it might not be able to rebuild itself, as it had in the days of its prosperity and vigor. To John Solum, though, the town's plight seemed to be just a painter's insoluble problem.

He asked, "Are you going home?"

"Yes." I hesitated. His company was the last thing I wanted. But it was a raw, cold night, as well as a disastrous one.

"Would you like to come in and have something warm to drink?"

"No, thanks. There's a boulder up ahead. From the top of it I ought to get a good view."

A good view of the flaming village.

The boulder stood only a few feet from the private road leading to the Fonsell house. As I turned down the road, I could hear the scrape of his shoe soles over the rough granite.

I entered the silent house. As I neared the second floor landing, Paul appeared in the open doorway of his room. "Liza's all right," he said quickly. "Not a sound out of her. But Ephraim's worse."

"Coughing?"

"And more feverish. I intended to go down to the village as soon as you came back, but—"

"There's no need to. Dr. Cantrell's there."

"Well, I guess I'll be sent for, if I'm wanted." He paused. "Did you find Jason?"

"Yes."

"Is the refinery . . ."

I said, in a dull voice, "He's tearing it down."

After a moment Paul said, "You mean, to stop the fire. Well, perhaps the town will pay for its rebuilding."

"Perhaps." The town had compensated the owner of a house razed during the 1845 fire. But the village would not, and probably could not, replace that expensive machinery, especially after the staggering loss it was sustaining tonight.

He said, "Did you see Ruth? I heard her go out after you did."

I told him of my conversation with her down at the bridge. He said, "A strange, strange girl," and I knew that he too felt that she was standing guard.

I said, "I'll look in on Liza. Good night, Paul."

Despite the sullen red light flickering at her window, Liza slept quietly. I closed her door and went to my room and

Jason's. Standing at the window, I felt a surge of pity and despair. On Bay Street, the fire had raged past the point where the refinery had stood. So Jason's sacrifice had been for nothing. The fire was still spreading. And if the wind changed, every wooden building on lower Main Street might go, and the houses along Captains' Row, and even Aunt Elizabeth's house on Howard Street . . .

Aunt Elizabeth. What would she do, instead of standing helplessly at this window? I knew. She would do what she always did when confronted with some trouble that neither her intelligence nor her energy could combat. She would go down to that room she had occupied and take up her heavy old Bible. Perhaps, as I had often seen her do, she would open the Bible at random, close her eyes, and place her finger on the page. Then she would read the verse chance had indicated. Many times, she told me, she had found comfort in that random choice. I left the room and went downstairs.

Even though I still wore my cloak, I found that first floor bedroom cold. With old newspapers and kindling from a small brass-bound chest that stood beside the fireplace, and coal from the scuttle, I built a fire in the grate. Then I lifted the heavy Bible from the bedside stand. As nearly as I could remember, I had never read from Aunt Elizabeth's Bible. After all, I had my own. But now I found comfort in just the smooth feel of it in my hand. I carried it over to one of the slipper chairs flanking the fireplace, sat down, and opened the Bible at its bookmark.

The verse I chose with closed eyes and randomly placed finger read: "And Balak said unto Balaam, Neither curse them at all, nor bless them at all." Even my aunt, I felt, would be hard put to find in those words anything applicable to this night.

I fingered the bookmark, a double thickness of leather about six inches long, with a gold-tooled thistle design. The strap's lower end felt bulky, as if something had been placed between the two layers of leather. Yes, the stitching had been unraveled at that end. Reaching in between the layers, I drew out a small sheet of thin paper, folded over many times.

The paper was yellowed, and brittle at the creases. The handwriting, faded to a light brown, was almost illegible. The dateline was London, November 3, 1836. The letter read:

My dear Miss Haverly,

Because I think so often of our pleasant discussions of the works of Mr. Gibbon and other authors, I have taken the liberty of sending you a small present. It is a music box, and it has a secret drawer! I am sure that such a clever young lady as yourself will find it.

To your sister I am sending an ivory fan. It is not without a sense of guilt that I do so. With her beautiful eyes flashing above it, she will wreak even greater havoc among the swains of Sag Harbor. Ah, Prudence, who provokes such imprudence in others!

I trust your esteemed father and mother are well. Although I do not plan to return to the States, I shall never forget the many pleasant hours I spent at their house on Howard Street.

I remain, my dear Miss Haverly,
                    Yr. Obedient Servant,
                    Henry Swindon.

I looked at the dateline again. London. In her last seconds of life, the only words my aunt's stricken brain had enabled her to speak were, "London. From London."

Now I knew why those words had reminded me of Aunt Prudence. In my memory she reclined on a sofa in the afternoon dimness of the Savannah house, reminiscing about her beaus. "One of them inherited money from an English relative and went to London to live. He'd been mad about me. I never heard such flowery love talk. Which was a pity, because I think your Aunt Elizabeth was rather sweet on him."

Rather sweet on him! She had loved him, that young man who had discussed Gibbon with her, and made impassioned speeches to her sister. She had loved him so much that she had kept his letter for forty years, in the bookmark of her cherished Bible. And that music box, which had sat on her dressing table for as long as I could remember, was one of the few belongings she had brought with her from the Howard Street house.

The music box. Was that what her dying brain had fumbled to express, something about that music box?

I laid the Bible and the yellowed letter on the fireplace mantel. Crossing the room, I picked up the music box and, careful not to lift the lid, began to press my fingertips over its top, sides, and bottom. With a suddenness that made me jump, a shallow drawer flew out from its apparently solid base.

The drawer held a small book, bound in red leather, about six inches long by four inches wide.

Dr. Cantrell had been wrong. I was sure of it. It wasn't a packet of letters which had made that dust-free rectangle beneath the loose board of the wardrobe floor. It was this book. Taking it from the little drawer, I set the music box on the dressing table and, heartbeats rapid now, returned to my chair and opened the small volume.

It was a diary. Not Aunt Elizabeth's. Before I had read more than a few sentences, I knew that this neat handwriting had been Julia Fonsell's. The first entry, dated September 15, 1860, read:

"Why I should start to keep a journal I don't know. Perhaps it is to convince myself that I am really alive.

"How self-pitying that sounds! I should be ashamed. After

all, I have my handsome little son. How many seven-year-olds show Steven's promise? Ephraim keeps me in comfort, and although he's rough-mannered, he's kinder, I'm sure, than many husbands. As for my stepson, he has never displayed the strong resentment I feared when I married Ephraim. For that, I know, I have his mother to thank. I doubt that she even knows the word philosophical, and yet she is a most philosophical woman.

"Perhaps it is Ruth who makes me so sad. School reopened today. It was almost impossible to get her out of the house. Tears, sobs, screams. And until that accident four years ago she was such a sunny little girl.

"Or perhaps it is this talk of a coming war that makes me sad.

"No! If I am to lie to myself, what is the use in keeping this journal? The chief source of my sadness is not my little daughter, nor fear of war with the southern states. Rather it is this. I was thirty-one yesterday. I do not love my husband, nor does he love me. He married me because, as he would phrase it, he wanted 'a fine-looking woman' to preside at his table.

"I have never known love. I will die without knowing it. That is why I am sad."

Raising my eyes from the page, I thought of the old man lying in feverish sleep in a room across the hall. I felt that Julia had been right about him. He had not loved her. Whenever he spoke of her to me it was without rancor, but also without tenderness. Nor had he seemed to mind that she had been, in his words, "a cold woman."

She had not written in her journal every day, or even every week. Sometimes an entry was dated a month later than the one preceding it. After those first melancholy paragraphs, the tone of the diary became matter-of-fact. She wrote of Ruth's measles, of Steven's whooping cough, of servants "let go" because of Ephraim's declining fortunes. There were references to "this terrible war," and to Union victories and defeats. Several times she expressed thankfulness that her husband was too old and her son far too young for the battlefield. An entry of February 25, 1865, read: "My stepson Jason volunteered today, his eighteenth birthday, but we hope that this cruel war will end before he is assigned to a regiment."

The entry for April 10, 1865, read: "It is over, thank God, it is over! General Lee surrendered yesterday." And then, less than a week later: "Tragic news. Last night Mr. Lincoln was assassinated."

Rapidly I skimmed accounts of flower gardening, of Ruth's excellent grades in her first-term report from the Misses Pride's school, of a sailing expedition on the Sound during which Ephraim caught a heavy chest cold. Then, from the entry for June 10, 1865, a name leaped out at me.

"Yesterday on Main Street we met a strange and fascinating man. A famous one, too. John R. Solum, the portrait painter. He walked up to Ephraim, presented his card, and asked us to have coffee with him at the Nassau House. It seems he wants to paint my portrait! Ephraim said in his blunt way that he couldn't afford it, and Mr. Solum said there would be no charge! Rich clients pay him enough, he said, that now and then he can paint someone 'for the pleasure of it.' Ephraim felt pleased and flattered, and I suppose I do too. I shall take the packet boat to New York each week until the portrait is finished. Already I have written to Cousin Louise Smathers, asking if I may stay at her house overnight whenever I am in New York. I am sure that her reply will be favorable.

"I wonder if all artists are as strange as Mr. Solum."

As strange as Mr. Solum. I thought of him out there on that boulder, staring at the conflagration, and seeing it, not as human disaster, but as spectacle—and unsatisfactory spectacle at that, since it was unpaintable.

Or was he still there?

With nameless unease, I turned to look at the French doors. Their draperies, I saw, did not quite meet. Rising, I laid the little book on the chair, and walked across the room. I made sure the doors were bolted, and drew the draperies together. Still that unease persisted. It would do no harm to bolt the already locked front and rear entrances. I could let Jason and Ruth in no matter at what hour they returned. There would be no sleep for me tonight.

I fastened the front door's bolt, and then moved along the silent hall, lighted only by one gas jet, turned low, and bolted the back door. After a moment's hesitation, I went into the kitchen and, aided by the flickering, dull red light that came through the window, found an oil lamp and matches on a shelf beside the stove. From the third floor I would get a comprehensive view of the village. Carrying the lighted lamp, I climbed the back stairs. On the second floor landing I looked down the hall, and saw that Paul's door was still partly open. Evidently he too wanted to hear Jason's return, and whatever news he brought.

From the window of an empty third floor room, I saw that most of Main Street was still unharmed. But the fire was far from conquered. The wind had driven the flames still farther west and south, along Bay Street and what appeared to be Rysam Street. I pictured Jason down there, trying not to think of his destroyed machinery as he held a hose some exhausted fireman had surrendered, or carried furniture out of some house in the path of the flames. Abruptly I turned from the window. There was nothing, nothing I could do, except wait to give him whatever comfort I could. I went downstairs, restored the oil lamp to its kitchen shelf, and returned to the coal fire and the little red book.

The next entry read: "I went to Mr. Solum's studio for my first sitting on Tuesday. Afterwards, tea at Delmonico's. It was wonderful, listening to a man who knows about painting and music. In fact, it was a little too wonderful. I know he expects us to spend more such pleasant hours. But we must not. Next time after the sitting I shall go straight to my cousin's house."

When she wrote again a week later, her handwriting had become less precise. "I am afraid I have no strength of character. Dinner, this time, and then a hansom cab through Central Park.

"Now that I have written such things here, I must hide this book. I will put it under the loose floorboard in my wardrobe.

"I have discovered that I am a weak person. But surely I am strong enough to send a letter saying that I intend to discontinue posing for my portrait. It is the only way to avoid temptation."

Apparently she had not been that strong. The next entry read, "Returned from New York today. I am ashamed, so terribly ashamed. It is almost impossible for me to look my husband and my children in the face. And yet I am happy, happy, happy!"

A week later she had written, "New York on Monday. Bliss. Returned home this evening."

As if she had been too preoccupied, or too filled with guilt, there were no entries at all for the next three weeks. Was it some time during those three weeks, I wondered, that Jason's mother had seen Julia and a man emerge from a New York hotel?

On the eighth of August she had written, "In New York last Tuesday I told him that now that the portrait is finished, we must never be together again like this. A terrible scene followed. I had not known he was capable of such rage."

I knew he was capable of it. I remembered how, the day that I had startled him, he had turned on me with a fury-contorted face, and hurled his paint-soaked brush onto the rug.

I raised my head, listening. No sound whatever, except the faint hiss of the gas light, and the measured tick of the clock in the hall. Why did I have this sense of danger drawing closer? The doors were locked. And anyway, why should he try to get in? He could not know that I sat here, reading of his love affair with a woman who, nearly twelve years ago, had met a brutal death in that garden beyond the locked and bolted back door. Just the same, that chill unease persisted, almost as if a cold wind was stealing through the open doorway into the hall, or beneath those bolted French doors behind me. I put more coals on the fire, and went on reading.

To my surprise, I saw my own name. "The portrait arrived this afternoon. It will be hung in time for Ruth's birthday party tomorrow." The names of the invited children followed, including my own.

"On Monday I will go to New York. I have told Ephraim that Cousin Louise Smathers has offered to give me singing lessons once a week. I am surprised that he believed me, because the lie seemed to stick in my throat, although why an adulteress should mind telling lies I don't know.

"And because I am an adulteress, I have had to submit to blackmail. Annabelle Clyssom knows that I have a lover. I should have realized that a woman like her would be sure to guess. For weeks now I have seen the knowledge in her eyes, her smile. And this morning she said, 'New York seems to do you so much good, Mrs. Fonsell. Maybe it would do Mr. Fonsell good to go with you. In fact, I've thought of suggesting it to him.' While I was searching my mind for some sort of reply, she said, 'You know that pendant you wore for your portrait? I've always just loved it. I'd be so grateful if I had a pendant like that.'

"I went straight to my room, and took the pendant from my jewel box, and handed it over to her."

I imagined Annabelle Clyssom's sense of triumph at that moment. Had it turned a little sour after Julia's death? Perhaps, but not enough so that she had given up possession of her ill-gotten ornament. I went on reading Julia's diary.

A week later she had written, "He insists that we must be together always, and I cannot hold out against him."

The next entry was dated September the fourth.

I stared at that date, half afraid to go on. Julia Fonsell had died the first week of that September.

"It is all arranged," she had written. "He will be waiting down at the cove at eleven tonight, with the small sloop he bought early last summer and left anchored at Noyack. We will cross the Sound to New London, and board a cargo-passenger ship that will sail for France early tomorrow morning.

"Strange, strange, to sit here on this sunny morning. I have lived in this house thirteen years. And now, in less than thirteen hours, I shall be leaving it forever."

The next paragraph was written in a hand so ragged that it almost looked like that of a different person. "It is now past nine o'clock. I should be packing the small valise that is all I intend to take with me, and putting this book inside it. And yet I sit here, paralyzed with indecision. I feel I cannot live without it, this love I had thought I would never have. I know that some women would give up everything—good name, husband, children—to follow such a love. But perhaps I am not selfish enough, or brave or reckless enough, to do that.

"What will he say, what will he do, if I go down there a little more than an hour from now, and tell him I have changed my mind?"

Even though there was still another paragraph written in that ragged hand, I raised my eyes from the page, sick with the knowledge of what must have happened. She had gone to the cove, told him of her new decision, and started back to the house. Perhaps it had taken a minute or so for his shock and frustration to turn to rage. But when it had, he had hurried after her, picking up that pine branch as he went. Inside the garden walls he had caught up with her, and brought down the club with such swiftness and force that she'd had no chance to cry out.

Did he still stand out there on that boulder in the darkness and February chill? I hoped he had gone now. Gone home to that Noyack cottage where, with incredible callousness, he had chosen to live, only a few miles from that walled garden back there.

I forced my gaze down to the final paragraph.

"Almost eleven now. I will put this journal in its hiding place, and then go down to the cove. I will tell him that I cannot leave my children, now or ever. He will argue that he is willing to sacrifice—sacrifice fine reputation, friends, practice. But I will be firm. I will come back here, kindle a fire in the grate, and burn this book."

But she had not been able to burn it. It had lain in its hiding place for almost ten years, until my aunt, stepping down off a footstool, had felt a loose board tilt under her foot.

Something wrong with a sentence in that final paragraph. I read it again. "He will argue that he is willing to sacrifice—sacrifice fine reputation, friends, practice." In her agitation, she must have written the wrong word. No one spoke of a painter's practice. You spoke of his career, or his work. Only lawyers and—

Swiftly, the book in my hand, I stood up. The thought that had come to me was absurd, so absurd that I could feel a rigid smile stretching my lips. Surely it was John Solum who had taken her to tea at Delmonico's after that first sitting. Her journal had said so. Or had it? Tomorrow I would reread it and make sure. But right now it might be just as well to restore this little book to the music box, and go quietly upstairs, and close my door.

Because, I thought, as I crossed the room, Paul must have

known Julia Fonsell. He had been Ephraim's doctor for fifteen years. No, it was seventeen years now. And just this evening he had mentioned his residency at a Brooklyn hospital "right after the War." One could imagine him crossing the East River by ferry one idle afternoon, and meeting by chance, on a Manhattan street, the beautiful and unloved wife of his irascible patient, and asking her to tea . . .

At the dressing table I paused, listening. No sound from upstairs. I could picture him standing, still fully dressed, at the window of his darkened room, watching the progress of the fire across the cove, and waiting for Jason's return. With fingers that had become cold and awkward, I replaced the journal in the little drawer, lifted the box, and began to feel over its surfaces for the hidden spring.

Behind me, a sound like a gunshot.

I whirled around. A second later I realized that it must have been a coal in the grate, bursting apart from the pressure of heated gas within it. But by then the harm had been done. The music box lay on the floor, its lid open, its trinket and the little red book scattered over the carpet. "O Christmas Tree," it played, its tinkled notes grotesquely joyous in the silent house, "O Christmas Tree!"

Bending, I closed the lid. Never mind the jewelry. Just get across the room and restore that diary to where it had lain undiscovered for so many years. No! Close the door into the hall first. I closed it. Carrying the book, I crossed the room, seized the knob of the wardrobe's right-hand door, tugged. It had stuck, as doors often did in the February damp. I tried the left-hand door. It would not budge. Dropping the book to the carpet, I pulled at the right-hand knob with both hands.

I did not hear him open the door behind me, or move over the thick carpet. I just heard him say, "Is anything wrong?"

Heart jumping, I turned around. It took two or three seconds, or perhaps a little longer, for his face to change, for the puzzled inquiry in his eyes to give way to shock, and then pain, and then a kind of dull despair.

He said, "Your aunt had the same look on her face that night."

For the first time since I had known him, he appeared to be his age. No, older. I said, with a smile I knew must look grotesque, "I don't know what you're talking about."

"I liked her," he said, as if I hadn't spoken. "I was sorry her headache kept her from the birthday dinner. So on my way out that night, I tapped on her door. She opened it, and I saw that—that horror leap into her face."

Unable to speak, I just looked at him. Surely he would not harm *me*, surely not. And yet twice before . . .

He went on, "I said something to her, I don't remember what, and she closed her door. But I knew she had guessed, somehow. And so before I went out through the garden, I left my bag on that bench near the back door."

So that if he met any of the rest of us when he came back later that night, he could say he had forgotten his bag. But he had seen no one except my frail little aunt, climbing the stairs.

As I stood there, numb, he bent, picked up the small book, and leafed through several pages toward the back. "So this was it," he said. His voice, like his eyes, was dull. "I knew there must be something. But when I searched this room—afterwards, I didn't find it.

"A diary," he went on after a moment, in that same dull voice. "That first afternoon in New York she told me she kept a diary. But later she told me she had stopped writing in it. Women," he said, and ripped the pages loose from their covers. He tossed them onto the grate, and the covers after them. Fascinated, I watched a page stir in the updraft, turn brown, burst into flame.

I looked back at him. His face had changed, hardened.

I said, past the hammering pulse in the hollow of my throat, "You'd better just go now. I'll never tell anyone."

It was a silly thing to say. He did not answer it. He just looked at me, a suffering determination in his face. With a weird detachment I thought, "How old he looks." Now I knew the meaning of the phrase, as old as sin.

No use in trying to dodge past him. No use in screaming. There was only a bedridden old man to hear me, and a little child. A child who must not even be frightened, let alone left without her mother. I said, trying to sound quietly reasonable, "You're a doctor. Don't you realize that there's—something wrong with you?"

"You mean insane," he said, in that flat voice. "No, not now. With Julia I was. Insane with rage and pain. But not with your aunt. And not—"

Not now, with me.

I felt cold sweat roll down my sides under my woolen dress, under my cloak. "Then if you're sane, you must know that you'll be caught, this time."

He shook his head wearily. "No, there's the fire."

Not understanding, I looked at the grate. Bits of the diary's thinned and blackened pages were swirling upward.

"I mean the fire in the village." A spasm crossed his face. "Oh, God, Irene! Why did you have to find out?" Then, again in that dull, tired voice, "When they find you over there tomorrow, they won't know what happened."

I understood then. I imagined myself, unconscious or already dead, hidden under a blanket in the rear seat of his surrey. He could drive across the bridge to the back entrance of some building already aflame, carry me inside, leave. In all that confusion—blinding smoke and roaring flame, embattled firemen, frightened, milling spectators—the chances were excellent that his presence would not be noticed, or, if noticed, remembered. And when questioned tomorrow, he could say that against his advice I had returned to the village to look for Jason. It would be a risk, yes. But not so great a risk as letting me live.

I thought, with a surge of rage so hot that it almost blotted out my fear, "But I'm going to live." For Liza, and Jason, and myself. I would not let him kill me, this man who had killed my wonderful aunt and, before her, pitiful, love-starved Julia Fonsell.

I saw his gaze go to the metal stand that held the fire tongs, the poker.

I moved then, bending to snatch up the coal scuttle, straightening to hurl it. He must have seen my movement, because he crooked one arm in front of his face. But by then I'd flung the scuttle and was racing toward the doorway into the hall. No time to unlock, unbolt the front door. I turned toward the stairs.

Perhaps the scuttle itself, or a chunk of flying coal, had staggered him momentarily, because I was almost halfway up the first flight before I heard him pounding after me. I turned at the landing, hating the encumbrance of my long skirts, my heavy cloak. The painter's ladder, I thought, leading up to the skylight. That ugly skylight with its protective steel mesh, propped open now lest it stick to the newly painted circle of wood upon which it ordinarily rested.

I started up the second flight, through darkness relieved only by a faint glow from the first floor hall. He was closer now, so close that I could hear not only the pounding of his feet, but his laboring breath. Before I could reach that ladder, I would feel his hands clutching my cloak, dragging me backward.

Something white ahead, there on the third floor landing. A large bucket, its sides coated with the paint it held. If I could reach it in time . . . Lungs agonized, I plunged up the last few steps, and with the side of my foot sent the paint bucket toppling down the stairs. I had already grasped the ladder's side rails when I heard his stumble, his sobbing curse.

I climbed, face upturned to the cold damp air swirling down through the opened glass dome.

Don't think about dislodging the stick that propped it open. Don't think about the heavy, steel-rimmed mass crashing down upon me. Just get through that opening.

Now I could make out the two-by-six propping the dome. There was room to get past it, of course there was room. I bent at the waist, reached out through the darkness with both hands. My stretching, groping fingers found rungs of the widow's walk railing, tightened around them. I drew myself partway through the opening, every inch of my flesh and bone aware of what that heavy dome would do if it closed upon me. Forced to turn onto my side now, I drew my bent knees, the tips of my shoes, carefully and with agonizing slowness, past that wooden prop.

The squeak of shoe soles on the ladder's rungs now. Rigid with fear that I would not be quick enough, I struck the wooden prop, knocking it inward, and snatched my arm back. The dome crashed down.

Safe. It had taken two strong men to raise that skylight, and a third to prop it. I was safe.

Chapter 22

I HUDDLED THERE, feeling my heart slow, and drawing cold damp air into my still laboring lungs. The night was not entirely dark. Even as I lay there, face turned away from the flaming village, I was aware of its flickering light. And I could hear a distant, almost continuous sound that must have been made up of the flame's roar, and the crash of burning timbers, and scores of shouting voices.

But no sound came from below. He was defeated. Even if he smashed the dome's glass, he could not break through its protective steel mesh. Nor could he reach this roof from the outside. There was no ladder tall enough anywhere on the premises. And he would not, I assured myself—banishing a terrible thought that had flashed across my mind—try to set this sturdy brick house on fire. The scattered North Haven residents, still awake on this terrible night, would rush over and extinguish the flames long before they could reach the roof. Nor need I fear that, out of vindictiveness, he would harm Liza or Ephraim. He was not vindictive, merely determined to preserve his own life, no matter how miserable that guilt-ridden life must seem to him sometimes in the watches of the night.

No, he would leave now, not only this house, but Long Island, if he could manage it. I pictured him hurrying down the staircase, back along the first floor hall. Even though I was sure of what he would do, my body went slack with relief when I heard the distant, grating sound of the back door's bolt. A few seconds later the hinges of the garden gate creaked. Then I could see him, a dark figure hurrying toward the carriage house. He disappeared inside. I wanted to get to my feet then, and look toward the village to see if Jason and all those others were losing or winning the battle. But no. Stay huddled. Wait until he was entirely gone.

He was driving out now, in the surrey which, on so many Wednesday afternoons, I had observed with pleasure as it approached the front steps. I huddled lower, listening to the sound of hoofbeats, of wheels grating over gravel, as he moved along the drive at the west side of the house.

The sounds stopped.

All my thoughts, even my heartbeats, seemed to stop too. I lay there, motionless. Then I heard the creak of metal, and I remembered it. The drainpipe. The wide drainpipe, with the strong iron clamps binding it to the brick wall. He was climbing up here. And later, although I would not know it by then, he would carry me down to the surrey, and cover me with the blanket I had so often seen neatly folded on the rear seat.

His face, a white blur in the darkness, appeared above the roof's edge. Even though I knew it was futile, insanely futile, I turned, hooked my fingers through that steel mesh, and tried to lift the dome. Then, abandoning the absurd effort, I let go of the mesh and turned to look at him. He had one knee on the roof's edge.

Throwing back my head, I let a scream rip from my throat. I went on screaming—wildly, despairingly—as he crawled toward me, propelled by his stockinged feet, advancing one flattened hand and then the other, up the roof's steep slope. He was only a yard or so away now. I went on screaming.

"Irene!"

Jason's voice, from down there on the drive.

"Jason! Jason!"

The crawling figure had halted. He turned his head toward the creaking sound of the drainpipe, and then tried to stand up on the ice-coated roof. I saw him topple heavily to one side as his feet slipped out from under him. And then he slid, clawing vainly at the shingles, and disapppeared over the roof's edge.

I got to my knees and clung, trembling, to the rail of the widow's walk. Jason had clambered onto the roof now. But there was something wrong with him. He propelled himself toward me on his elbows. "It's all right, darling," he said. "It's all right."

I could see now why he crawled upward on his elbows, and why he'd had to retreat from the battle in the village. The swollen hands he held in the air looked black in that light, but I knew that they must be raw and blistered and bleeding.

A distant voice called from somewhere beyond the front of the house. "What was all that screaming? You got trouble in there?"

Jason turned his head toward the voice. "Yes!" he shouted. "On the roof. We need help." Then to me: "It's all right. We'll be all right."

But his words came to me faintly through the roaring sound, through the blackness, closing in around me.

Chapter 23

I WAS STILL unconscious when three North Haven men climbed to the roof, managed to open the dome, and lowered it back upon its rusted hinges. I remained unconscious as one of them carried me down the ladder to Jason's room and mine. When I came groggily to my senses I lay, still wearing my cloak, on the bed. Beside me stood a small but wiry man whom I recognized as Bert Crenson, a North Haven dairy farmer.

He held out a glass filled with cloudy liquid. "Your husband says for you to drink this."

I hoisted myself onto my elbows. "Where is—"

"Jason looked in on the little girl. She's all right. Now my brother is bandaging his hands. Drink this."

"What is it?"

"Some kind of nerve medicine. Your husband told me where to find it in the old man's room. Drink it."

I drank it.

I came awake in the early morning light to find someone unbuttoning my cloak. It was Ruth, bending over me with that faint smile. When she saw that my eyes were open she said, "The fire's out."

I looked up at her silently, my mind still cloudy with the sedative. "I guess about a hundred buildings burned." Sliding an arm under me, she raised me from the pillow and pulled the cloak from my shoulders. "But all but the lower part of Main Street was saved. And it never got near the bridge.

Jason says I'm to help you undress. He couldn't. His hands are too bad."

"Liza?"

"Mrs. Johansen is giving her breakfast."

I got dizzily to my feet. With Ruth's help I undressed, put on my nightgown, and got back into bed. I asked, "Where is Jason?"

"Down in the village. Everybody is, looking over the ruins." She had her hand on the doorknob before I could force myself to ask, "And—Paul Ronsard?"

"He's at Dr. Cantrell's house. Bert and Harry Crenson took him there last night." She smiled her eerily inappropriate little smile. "Maybe he's dead now. Jason said his back seemed to be broken," she said, and left the room.

I must have slept again for several hours, because when a tap on the door awoke me, the morning sun had withdrawn from the windows. "Come in," I called.

Dr. Cantrell moved toward me. The bedside chair creaked under his weight. "How do you feel?"

"All right." I ached in every muscle, but my mind was clear. "Who are those people downstairs?" I could hear men's voices, apparently coming from the dining room.

He smiled. "I'm sure the newspaper, in its next edition, will call them a delegation of leading citizens. They've come to see Jason."

I looked at him, waiting.

"That was a damned fine thing Jason did last night." He was not smiling now. "A futile thing, since it didn't stop the fire. But nevertheless, a fine thing. People appreciate it."

Feeling a tightness in my throat, and the sting of tears in my eyes, I turned my head away. Then I looked back at him. "And Paul Ronsard?"

"He's dead, poor devil. He died about five this morning. He was conscious right up until the end, and he talked and talked. Sometimes it was pretty confused and rambling, but

I think I managed to piece the story together." He paused. "Ronsard was the one who attacked you that evening in your aunt's house."

"I realize he must have been. But I don't understand why."

"It seems Ephraim overheard a quarrel between you and Jason. You made some threat about going to the hotel on Fourteenth Street in New York. Ephraim told Ronsard about it when Ronsard arrived the next afternoon."

Of course, I thought. In the past it had been apparent that Ephraim discussed everything with his doctor, even, to Jason's annoyance, details of Jason's business affairs. And that night at dinner, even though I could not recall doing so, I had probably mentioned that I was going over to the Howard Street house the next day.

"Ronsard was scared. You see, he knew that the manager of that Fourteenth Street hotel remembered him. Just last spring, when Ronsard went to a medical convention in New York, he ran into the manager in a restaurant. The manager not only recognized him. He called him by the name Ronsard had used whenever he and Julia Fonsell registered at that hotel."

And so, Dr. Cantrell said, Paul Ronsard had gone over to the Howard Street house that night and waited for me. I could imagine how, after I arrived late the next afternoon, he had gone through an emotional struggle down there on the increasingly dark second floor, not wanting to bludgeon me as he had bludgeoned Julia Fonsell, and yet afraid not to. Finally, when I had started to run for help, he had realized that he must strike.

Dr. Cantrell said, "Unlike poor Julia, you had a chance to scream."

"And that frightened him off."

"I think it horrified him even more than it frightened him. He said to me, 'I guess I was a little out of my head, because it seemed to me it was the first time, and that it was Julia who was screaming.' Anyway, he left the house by that kitchen window, and went over to the far end of Redwood, where he had left his horse and surrey in some thick woods. Then he went home."

And later, when I made no move to go to New York, but instead started to arrange to sail on the *Kestrel,* he came to feel that I represented no threat to him.

Had he ever really loved me, or at least thought he did? Or had he decided that if he married me, and took me away somewhere, there would be almost no chance that I would ever learn more about the two sudden deaths in this house? Probably, I decided, it had been a mixture of reasons which impelled his proposal in that San Isidro garden.

"It's hard for me to understand him," I said slowly. "He seemed so patiently kind and generous. The night I met him, he told me that he'd been calling on Ephraim every Wednesday for the last five years."

"That puzzles you? Now? It used to puzzle me. I wondered why he lavished his time and skill on a drunken old man. But now I understand why. He must have felt it was some sort of—expiation, putting up with the bad-tempered old husband of the woman he had murdered."

He cocked his head, listening. "Sounds as if they are breaking up down there. Well, I'll go down and say a few words to Jason, and then get back to my office."

Perhaps five minutes passed before Jason came in. His dark face held such a blend of embarrassment and pleasure that again I felt a tightness in my throat. He kissed me and then sat in the bedside chair, his bandaged hands resting on his knees.

"I'll get up in a few minutes," I said. "I just feel lazy." Then I added, "I hear the town is working on a laurel wreath for you."

His smile, happy and a touch sheepish, made him look very young. "Something like that."

I asked, after a moment, "What are you going to do, Jason? About the refinery, I mean."

"Nothing."

"Nothing!"

"I'm not going to rebuild, or buy new machinery. I haven't the money. And even though people might back me now, I wouldn't want them to. It would be too risky. The *Kestrel* will bring us enough. We'll never be rich, but we'll get by."

I understood. He no longer felt he had to make us rich, or create a booming industry for the town. Those men today had given him what he had wanted all his life.

And the houses, I thought, with an inward smile, those gracious houses on Captains' Row. Maybe now they would never be replaced by stone mansions with cupolas, and iron deer on the lawns. Maybe they would be there for our children to admire, and their children. And maybe, after a while, enough people would come to enjoy the sight of them that no one would dream of tearing them down.

"Oh, Jason," I said. "We'll get along fine, just fine."

And because I couldn't hold his bandaged hand, I ran my hand up my husband's sleeve and held his arm, tight.